WITHDRA

NOV   '75

JUN   1992

AUG '88

JAN '83

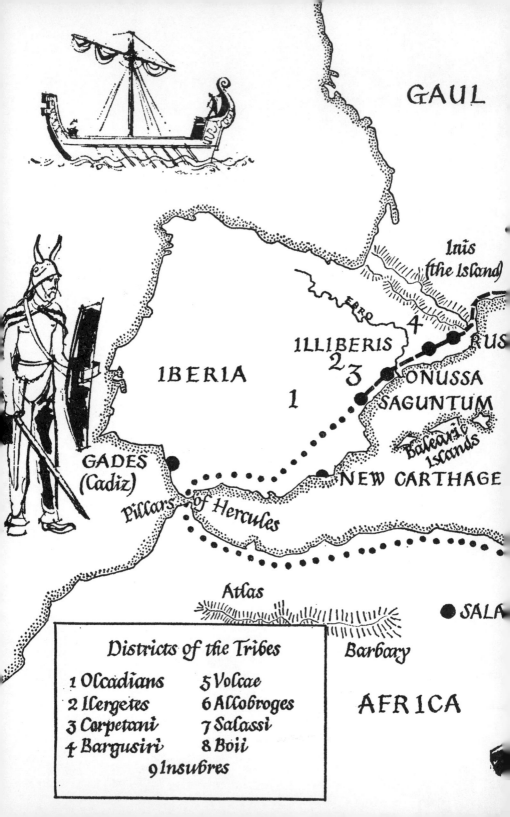

GAUL

Inis
(the Island)

EBRO

4

ILLIBERIS

2 3 ...RUS

1

ONUSSA

IBERIA

SAGUNTUM

Balearic Islands

GADES
(Cadiz)

NEW CARTHAGE

Pillars of Hercules

Atlas

● SALA

Barbary

AFRICA

Districts of the Tribes

1 Olcadians   5 Volcae
2 Ilergetes   6 Allobroges
3 Carpetani   7 Salassi
4 Bargusiri   8 Boii
        9 Insubres

Alps

Town of the Taurini (TURIN)

PLACENTIA (PIACENZA)

MASSILIA
(MARSEILLES)

NO *Lake Trasimenus*

ROME

CANNAE

GREECE

Sardinia

ERYS

MESSINA

ATHENS

MEGARA   CARTHAGE   SYRACUSE

ZAMA

umidia

N
W   E
S

━━ Hannibal's Great March
••• Suru's Journey Home

I Marched With
HANNIBAL

I Marched With

HANNIBAL

HANS BAUMANN

Translated by
Katharine Potts

Illustrated by
ULRIK SCHRAMM

New York
HENRY Z. WALCK, INC.

First published 1960 under the title
Ich zog mit Hannibal
by Ensslin & Laiblin Verlag Reutlingen
© Ensslin & Laiblin Verlag Reutlingen 1960

English translation
© Oxford University Press 1961

First American Edition 1962

Library of Congress Catalog Card Number : 62-16055

Printed in Great Britain by Richard Clay (The Chaucer Press), Ltd.,
Bungay, Suffolk

CONTENTS

The Treasure-Seeker

Tana and Morik had been fetching water. The girl and her brother were each carrying half of the pack-saddle which had belonged to the donkey who had survived the flight with them. He had trotted to the well with it on his back and had held out for nearly a year. Then they had buried him under dried pellets of earth. Their father had cut the saddle into two pieces and made each piece to fit on to the children's shoulders. For a whole year it had been their work to fetch water. At least twice every day they followed the path which they and the donkey had made, at dawn and towards evening, when a red hole was to be seen in the sky above the tops of the western mountains, a hole which grew bigger before it went down behind the mountains. There were days when the jugs were empty by midday, and then they had to go a third time, when the sun was over the sea and the sea glittered so fiercely that it hurt their eyes. The path scorched the soles of their feet, and Tana and Morik wrapped cloths round their heads, particularly in July and August.

Now it was the beginning of October. The sun changed itself into the large round hole in the west earlier than in August, and it poured out a red light over the burnt land.

'Now it doesn't hurt our eyes any more,' said Tana.

Morik was not looking at the sun; he was looking straight ahead.

'If he's digging there again today, we shall see him very soon,' he said, beginning to walk faster.

Tana let her brother get ahead. He was twelve, she was nearly fourteen, and she could not get out of the habit of looking after him, although he had grown so much during the past year that he was already taller than she. She was always afraid that the heavy water-carrying might one day be too much for him. The tall jugs which narrowed down to a point and fitted into the halves of the saddle were filled to the brim, and they dragged on the children's shoulders. The stirrups hung down in front over their chests, and Tana and Morik pushed their arms through the stirrups so that their elbows could take the weight. It took them nearly an hour to walk to the well. Nowhere but at the fort was it possible to get good water. The way to it cut right through the town. Tana and Morik walked on top of the houses because that was simpler than following the streets. The streets were hidden under broken bricks and ashes. The whole town, once a large settlement near the coast, had been levelled to the ground. It had been done so thoroughly that the houses had turned into rubbish heaps and their cellars into caves. For two whole years Tana and Morik had lived with their father and mother in one of these caves.

Their 'house' had been allotted to them by the men who were now masters in the land, a house and a piece of land bigger than the fields they had lost. About a hundred families had escaped with their bare lives from the barbarian invasion, and these the Romans had brought to this point on the south coast of the Iberian province. They wanted the dead town to be brought back to life again. But when the fugitives saw that there was only rubbish instead of houses, that the fields and gardens had turned into wilderness and that the cisterns were lying choked in the mud, many had refused on the spot to set their hands to the work, and those who had made the attempt had wandered away again during the first year, all except nine or ten families. These few did not stay behind for the sake of the poor crops which the fields yielded, nor for the harvest of the seashore. They had fastened on the rubbish heaps and begun to dig secretly in the night-time. They held obstinately to the rumour that during the siege of the town all the gold and silver had been collected and buried in a shaft which had been covered in by an iron-bound trap-door, and that this trap-door was hidden under rubbish. During the first year these treasure-seekers had dug night after night in the ruins. First there had been nine or ten of them, then five, then three, and lastly only one.

2

This one had been trying for more than two years, and Tana and Morik had helped him on many a night—until a week ago. They had found nothing but mouldering refuse.

'It's a good thing that Father's going to give up,' said Tana.

Morik was standing still. 'Look! He's still digging at the same spot; he's been digging there three days,' he whispered. 'And he does it in broad daylight.'

He had no need to whisper for the sake of the man whom he saw digging. The man was far enough away.

'What business is it of ours?' Tana tried to make him go on.

'It's very much our business,' Morik maintained. 'He's digging where he's no right to dig—so near us!'

'We've never dug there,' Tana objected.

'That's just it!' said Morik obstinately. 'We must begin to dig there now.'

'But Father doesn't want to go on,' Tana objected. 'He thinks that he earns enough from fishing, now that he's giving his whole time to it. Go on!'

Morik did not move. He was watching the digger, and Tana also looked at him, more carefully now. She saw how slowly he bent down, how heavy each single stone that he lifted seemed to be. His face and beard were red from the reflection of the sun. He must be a very old man. He moved the stones which he lifted out of the rubbish a little to one side and was beginning to build them into a wall.

'He's going to build a house,' said Tana; 'an old man like that!'

Morik gave her a pitying look. 'He's only pretending to be doing it for the sake of the stones. He's digging like a man who knows very well where it's worth his while to dig. We mustn't keep it secret from Father any longer.'

Tana tried to dissuade him. 'Don't worry Father with that. He's made himself a boat and wants to give up digging.'

'As soon as he hears about this he'll begin again,' Morik answered her. And now he walked on so fast that Tana could hardly keep pace with him. He turned aside from the path because he didn't want to walk close by the old man. He walked

3

round the mound which separated the digger from the cave in which they lived. After a few hundred steps they saw smoke. It could only be coming out of their cave. There was a smell of fried fish.

'It makes you thirsty,' said their father when his children arrived. He was turning two scorched rods from which fishes were dangling. The fire had made his face much brighter than usual.

'You've come just at the right moment.' He looked like a man who has made a good catch, and their mother held up a pail with glittering fish in it.

'It's quite settled now,' said she, 'we're going to move down to the sea. Father has found a spring of water, a good place for a house. . . . Is anything the matter with you?' She looked anxiously at Morik.

Morik did not meet her eyes; he looked at the fire instead.

'Don't tell them!' whispered Tana.

'What isn't he to tell?' asked their father.

'Someone is digging quite near us,' Morik confessed.

At that their father put down the rods on which the fish were roasting as suddenly as if they had burnt his fingers. 'Has one of them come back?'

'It isn't anyone who came with us,' Morik told him. 'It's a stranger; he must be very old, and he's been digging for three days—in broad daylight.'

'And you didn't tell me?' Their father spoke angrily.

Tana defended herself. 'You didn't want to dig any more.'

'We didn't even see him coming, he was just there,' said

4

Morik; 'and he doesn't dig as if he were in a hurry but like a man
who knows that it will be worth his while in the end.'

Their father wanted to go at once to see the man, but their
mother held him back. She pointed to the fish. 'It was a good
beginning,' she said.

'Even by the sea we shall only just keep starvation at bay,' said
their father. 'If someone really is digging we won't go away.'
He took Morik by the arm. 'An old man, did you say?'

'He must be very old,' Morik repeated.

'Then he might really know something.' Now their father's
face looked as if it had caught fire. 'Come, Morik, we'll go
along.'

5

'It would be better if Tana and I went,' Morik suggested. 'If you go, he'll only try to pretend he's building a house.'

'I'll soon deal with him,' said their father threateningly. 'Whatever possessed him to think he could begin to dig just outside our front door?' Then he stopped and thought for a moment. And when Tana took up the argument and said, 'Maybe he will think Morik and I might be useful to him; I've noticed how heavy the work is for him,' their father agreed that the two children should go.

'But don't let him deceive you!' he warned them.

Morik was hunting about in the corner where the digging tools were kept.

'First you must eat,' their mother insisted, 'and when you do go, take a jug with you; he will certainly be thirsty.'

Morik ate hurriedly. Tana too did not let the meal delay her long. As they went off Morik said, 'Don't be anxious if we don't come back for a while. Perhaps he digs all through the night, as we used to.' In one hand he was carrying a pickaxe, in the other a basket; Tana took one of the two jugs. They climbed out of the cave. Morik walked in front as he did on the way to the well. When they had come round to the other side of the mound they saw the old man in front of them. He looked up when he heard them coming and put the stone which he was holding down on to the low wall which he had already built. He made no haste.

'How good that you've brought water with you,' he said. 'I need that more than anything.' He spoke to the two children as if they were old acquaintances. 'You live next door?'

'We have lived there for more than two years,' Tana explained.

'I'm only just beginning on my house,' the old man told them confidingly.

'We might help you,' suggested Tana.

'You have come in the nick of time,' he admitted. 'I have neither pickaxe nor basket. It isn't easy with the hands, particularly when—like mine—they aren't good for much.' He pointed to the wall he had begun to build. 'That's going to be my house.'

'A house?' Morik asked suspiciously. 'Don't pretend you're only digging for stones!'

The old man raised his eyebrows. 'You are right,' he said, 'the stones are only a beginning. It's good that you've brought a pickaxe. The important thing is deeper down.'

Morik kept his eyes on him the whole time. He was looking at a face whose skin reminded him of the bark of old trees. It had countless little hollows.

'Are you at home here?' Morik was determined to stand his ground.

The old man nodded. 'I know every inch of the ground. If it's worth while digging anywhere, then it's worth while here. Let's begin!'

The hole he had made was already three steps deep. Morik went down them and began to dig. When it grew dark the old man made a fire. He had collected a little stock of dried branches, and although he was very sparing with them, the firelight reached the bottom of the hole in which Morik was standing, first up to his knees, then up to his hips and finally up to his chest. When the basket was full he handed it up to Tana, and the old man picked out the stones that he could use. Tana carried the rubble away; she emptied the basket on to a heap. When they rested for a few moments in order to drink, the old man picked up two stones and looked at them carefully. 'These are both old acquaintances,' he assured them, and when Morik looked at him doubtfully, he said, 'It won't be long now before you strike iron.'

Half an hour later Morik's axe-stroke made a ringing sound. He threw the pickaxe down and raked the rubble with his hands. 'Try again with the pickaxe!' the stranger said. 'It won't hurt the door.'

Morik struck again, and this time again iron met iron and this time the sound was hollow.

'We're through,' said the old man. 'We were on the right track.'

He let Morik dig two more steps out of the rubble, then he went down himself into the hole, crouched down on his heels, removed some smaller stones with his hands, blew the last remains of soil away from the surface he had exposed, and then asked them to hand him down a branch which was sticking out of the fire. He pointed the burning end down into the hole almost to the bottom. Morik and Tana could see some rusty iron bands. It was not long before Morik had cleared all the rubble away from the trap-door.

'Is it down there?' asked Morik and Tana both together.

They saw the old man's eyes shining.

'It was there when I went away,' he said, 'and it must be there now, even after sixty years. Who could have dug it up? There's no one else left who could have known the place.'

Morik wanted to open it at once.

'Not while it's still dark,' the old man insisted.

'Why not now?' Morik took hold of the rusty ring on the door.

Then the strange man raised his face. 'I want to see it sparkling down there when we open the shaft.' He climbed out of the hole with the glowing branch.

'But what are we to do now?' asked Tana, disappointed.

'I would be glad to give you something to eat,' said the old man with some embarrassment, 'but I have nothing left. Come back early tomorrow morning!'

Morik was staring at the rusty iron fittings. Now he exchanged a knowing look with Tana.

The look did not escape the old man. 'I'm not trying to get rid of you,' he assured them. 'There's more than enough down there, not only for us three. If you hadn't come to me I should have come to you. It would have been the only thing I could do to save myself from starving.'

Morik could not bring himself to leave the hole. But Tana gave a start when the old man talked of starving. 'I'll be back soon,' she said, and she ran off.

Then the old man sat down with his back to the low wall and stretched out his feet towards the fire. 'Come and sit by me,' he said to Morik. 'It's warmer here.'

8

The boy moved up towards him unwillingly. Across the fire, which had burnt low, he looked at the stranger. The old man pushed a dry branch into the glow and it blazed up.

'You have been digging too?'

'We've managed to hold out for more than two years,' answered the boy, 'but it's not possible to live here.'

'Things will be different now,' the stranger promised him. He looked closely at Morik. 'Why don't you trust me?'

'How do I know who you are?' the boy asked with a hard look on his face. The old man seemed not to hear the reproach.

'You've been through too much,' he said, 'and what can I say?' He fell silent and looked at the fire.

Morik studied his heavily lined face. He tried to guess how old the man was. Perhaps seventy, he thought. He felt there was something uncanny about this stranger who sat there in his ragged clothes but was not at all like a beggar.

'It's a good thing you stayed,' said the old man. 'Now you don't need to go away.'

'At first we weren't the only ones digging,' said Morik. The hardness in him was beginning to thaw. 'There were nine or ten of us, and each man was the other's enemy and each kept a watch on the other. But no one found anything. We often dug right through the night. When Father heard that you were digging here he wanted to come and see.'

'I was expecting him,' said the old man. 'We are neighbours.'

'He wanted to say you had no right to the place and that it was his,' Morik explained.

The old man took it quite calmly. 'There's enough for us all,' he said for the second time and pushed the branch which was now blazing right into the fire. Soon after Tana came back. She was carrying a large wooden plate with bread and two fishes on it.

'This was left over,' she said and handed the plate to the stranger.

'Why didn't your father come with you?' the old man asked. 'Didn't you tell him?'

9

'No,' said Tana. 'He'll find out tomorrow. He thinks we're still digging.'

'I haven't had anything to eat since early this morning,' the old man apologized as he helped himself. The fish tasted good. He drank some water and was going to pass the plate round. 'Divide the second fish between you. Don't let it slip through your fingers—it might, you know!'

Tana refused. 'We have eaten.' She liked watching the old man eating and enjoying the food. When he had finished both the fishes Morik returned to the attack: 'Why can't we open it up now? Just one look into the shaft!'

'Not before tomorrow morning,' the stranger insisted. 'I want to see it sparkling down there.'

'We can light up the shaft with a burning branch,' Morik suggested.

'That wouldn't make a proper sparkle,' the old man persisted obstinately. Then he began to rack his brains. 'What have I got that I could give you?' He beat his breast. 'You have helped the old fellow—never mind what your reasons were. You brought him food. He doesn't like to think that he is boring you.' For a while he raked about in the fire as if he were looking for something. Then he looked up and said surprisingly, 'We might dig!'

'But that was just what you didn't want to do,' said Morik.

'Not there in the hole,' the old man explained. 'Here!' He beat his breast again. 'There's something in there that you wouldn't be likely to guess.' He screwed his eyes up so tightly that you could only see two slits. 'It sounds mad, but I know what I am saying. There's an elephant in there. He's called Suru. How do you like the name?'

Tana and Morik looked at him in amazement. They were not sure whether to take the question seriously.

'I know what I'm saying,' the old man repeated. 'Suru is in there. We've been connected with one another ever since I was a boy. We didn't spend a day apart from one another. At first I marched with the elephant and then he marched with me. We

10

belonged to that company of men who went on the long march
from here to the high mountains that are never free of ice, and
then over the mountains, on and on until we came to the gates of
Rome.'

'You were on Hannibal's march?' asked Morik, beside himself
with excitement.

'It began here,' said the old man. 'Suru carried me away from
here, and I came back here with him.' He looked about him in
the darkness. 'And after all these years nothing but ruins—not
one stone above another.' He looked at Morik. 'How old are
you? Twelve? I was no older than you are now when Saguntum
was destroyed. There I lay—only a few steps away, unable to

move because I was half buried. All round me the houses were falling down. The whole town was on fire. The fiery breath singed my eyebrows and hair. And then in the middle of the fire night fell for me; I don't know how long it lasted.' The old man was leaning down over the fire; Tana and Morik saw the flames in his face.

'And did no one pull you out?' asked Tana.

'There was no one there,' the old man explained. 'Those who weren't dead were driven away like cattle, and that was worse than being dead. The town was dead, and I lay there so still that the strangers who were over-running the town thought I was dead. Suru was the only one who didn't make that mistake. He, the elephant, who might have killed me with a single footstep, raised his enormous foot again almost before he had touched my shoulder. The touch was just enough to bring me back to my senses.'

Tana looked at him in alarm. 'An elephant trod on you—and you are still alive?'

'No elephant plants his foot down if he feels something alive under it,' the old man assured her. 'When I came to myself I saw a grey mountain, and it was alive. The elephant had only one tusk, and he held out this tusk and his trunk towards me. The expression in his eye as he looked at me gave me courage. As long as the town was being attacked, there had been nothing more dreadful for us than the gigantic machines with which they had rammed our walls. The elephant who had appeared so unexpectedly before me roused no fear in me. On the contrary, I thought: Nothing more can happen to me. My head didn't think this thought—it came out of my heart, which was beating so violently that I felt it in my throat.

'The driver had got down from the elephant so that he could see better what there was to be seen. He saw me. He was one of those who had been sent into the town to pick up any survivors. He was not a young man. A scar ran from his forehead right across his left cheek as if his face had been struck by lightning. I *was* afraid of him. Then the elephant touched him with his one remaining tusk and the driver turned round. I heard him asking Suru a question. Then he nodded as if the elephant had made him understand something, picked me up out of the rubble and took me with him. That was so many years ago that I've given up counting them.'

'And where have you been all this time?' asked Tana.

'On the way to Saguntum.'

'To Saguntum? Not to Rome?' asked Morik bewildered. 'Surely you were marching with the Carthaginians!'

'You are right, I marched with them to Rome,' the old man agreed. 'Suru was one of the elephants who crossed the Alps with Hannibal. He was the only one who got through in the end and I with him. I saw Rome and I even got as far as Carthage. I saw Saguntum burnt a second time.'

'Saguntum—not Carthage?' The old man's story was mystifying Morik more and more at each turn, and he was beginning to suspect him again.

'For me it was Saguntum,' the stranger declared. 'In the end there was as little left of Carthage as there was of Saguntum. In the midst of the ruins of Carthage I was overcome by homesickness, and it drove me back here.'

'And Suru?'

'What happened to the elephant?'

The old man struck his breast with his fist a third time. 'Since he first engaged in his great adventure I have never left him.' He picked up a bough, broke it in the middle, and thrust one half of it into the fire. 'Come closer,' he said, 'the night is getting chilly.' He propped himself up against the wall. 'It has often been told how the Carthaginian army crossed the Alps with the elephants. Even today there are people who talk about it. I was with the elephants till the end. Hannibal's elephant carried me.' He was silent for a little while; then he started up out of his dream. 'I came home in rags, with empty hands. That cannot be denied. But one thing they can't take from me: I was there. I took part in the great march of the elephants. I marched with Hannibal. Come closer!'

Tana and Morik moved as close up to him as the fire would let them. They had forgotten about the hole in the ground not five steps away. To begin with, there was nothing to hear but the fire. Then the old man drank out of the jug which was standing beside him and began his story.

The Great March of the Elephants

I

WHEN the Carthaginians began the siege of Saguntum I was twelve years old. I was too young to understand what was going on round me. Until then Saguntum had been a town where life had been good, even for those who lived from hand to mouth, as the saying is. Saguntum was by the sea and had a harbour. You could walk to it from the South Gate of the city in half an hour. The road to the coast led through gardens and fields which bore rich fruit, because they were protected by the mountains from the north wind. But the riches which were being piled up in the palaces did not come from the fields and gardens, but from the sea. Saguntum was a town to which the sea brought many ships. As far as anyone could look back it had been so. But now, from one day to the next, the town had turned into an island, and wave after wave rushed mercilessly against it until the island went down in a sea of flames. Who could expect a boy of twelve to understand such things?

Even before that time things had happened that I couldn't understand. In former years ships bound for Saguntum had sailed from Carthage also. They had brought pitchers. Now suddenly in the streets of our town men began to speak ill of the Carthaginians and to talk of the Punic plague which was devastating our coasts. Two town councillors who had been agents for the Carthaginians had been seized by the others, dragged to the city wall and flung down from it. It was said that messengers had been sent to the Romans in the hope that they would cover our rear. And then the rumour spread like wildfire from one city gate to the other: Hannibal is coming! I saw pale faces.

I knew who Hannibal was: one of the sons of that Carthaginian general who had conquered Iberia as far as the Ebro and made it into a Punic province. This Hamilcar Barca had left our town in peace. *Barca* means *lightning*, so they told me. The lightning had not struck us. But now his son Hannibal was marching against Saguntum, and he had more men than there were men, women, and children in the town.

He was called the Young Lightning. And this lightning was going to strike us. The army which he had on the march had come out of the mountains in the west like an enormous serpent which had a beginning but no end, and it wormed its way between the coast and the town and crept round the walls. Everything changed from one day to the next. Where fields and gardens had been there was now a wilderness. The serpent wormed its way into the fields and soon there was not a tree left standing. But the smoke of fires rose up all round the town, and in the night it looked as if Hell was beginning to break through the surface of the earth at more places than one could count.

I could not believe that it was human beings who were doing this. Did the men out there not know that a tree bears fruit? Didn't they feel hungry and eat what grows in the fields? Didn't they know how much trouble it takes to cultivate a field? After they had spread themselves out outside the walls they began to advance. The men in front were hidden under roofs which ran along on wheels.

'They're coming with rams and scorpions,' said my father, at whose side I was standing on the wall. I could see neither rams nor scorpions but monstrous things made of iron and wood which were threatening the walls. 'Now go!' said my father, and he picked up the weapons that were lying beside him. As I went I gave him one more look and what I saw frightened me. He no longer looked like my father; he had the face of a stranger. The hatred he felt for the men outside there had distorted his features. The look on his face made me afraid of him.

Where my father was standing the wall jutted out towards the sea and the ground fell away. This was the place where Hannibal planned to break his way into the town. He ordered hurling-engines and battering-rams to be brought to the spot, so that by their discharge of rocks and logs studded with huge nails the walls might be loosened. From the walls a hail of spears and arrows showered down on to the invaders. Stones were hurled down and made holes in the roofs under which the Carthaginians had felt safe. The defenders had spears with shafts made of pinewood, and out of them stuck iron spikes the length of half a man's arm. The spikes were wrapped round with tow, which was set alight before the spear was thrown. It broke out into flames in the air and was ablaze when it struck the shields of the men below.

But not only the ranks of the Carthaginians were growing thinner. Soon there were not enough men on the walls either. We half-grown boys brought them what they needed: food, weapons, stones, spears, and arrows, and this had often to be done when the battle was in full fury. Some boys too were hit. Several times I saw men pointing in horror to someone out there and I heard them shout: 'There he is, the new Barca!' And I saw a man in a red cloak who walked about out there as if no harm could come to him. Once he was only thirty steps away, and his cloak was so red that it looked like a flame shining in a dark night. He urged his soldiers on and was quite untroubled by the spears and arrows. Suddenly he put his hand to his hip; the flame wavered and collapsed as if a violent gust of wind had struck it. Three or four Carthaginians ran up and carried the man in the red cloak away. From the walls a cry went up: 'That's the end of him, the son of Moloch!' And a troop of our men, seized by the general intoxication, broke out of the South Door and wrought havoc in the disordered ranks of the enemy, until African horsemen spurred towards them and mowed them down.

In a week's time the man in the red cloak was to be seen again out there. We had not seen the last of him. He ordered his men to bring up a tower made of wood, which was taller than the stone towers of the town and which approached the wall on rollers. The tower had a roof which jutted far out. From the roof

18

four tree trunks hung by enormous chains. They struck the wall with their heavy iron plates at four different places at once, one above the other. The wall groaned, then roared, and at last collapsed. The monster tower turned slowly and rolled a hundred paces farther along the wall. The helpless defenders had to watch a second breach being made. And then the wooden tower advanced against one of the stone towers and knocked it down. After that the Carthaginians began to storm the town. But they found themselves up against walls that were bristling with blazing spears, which instead of giving way hurled themselves at the invaders. Then the Carthaginians retreated, leaving many lying dead on the battlefield. But the breaches in the wall did not repair themselves, and the town lay fatally exposed to attack. It lay in a pincer-grip that grew tighter and tighter.

Then a man ran over from Saguntum to the Carthaginians and offered to carry Hannibal's conditions for raising the siege back into the town. The conditions were hard: The men of the town with their wives and children were to leave Saguntum, each taking one garment. Everything else was to be left for the victor. The people of Saguntum were to build themselves a new town a three hours' journey inland from the sea.

The mediator returned to the town. A great crowd surrounded him and listened to what he had to say. But when he had said his last word their heaped-up bitterness found vent. The man was thrown down from the wall as the two town councillors had been who had spoken for the Carthaginians. The rich folk, beside themselves with rage at the conditions, collected their gold and silver and threw it into the shaft so that their treasure should not fall into the hands of the Carthaginians. Chests, cabinets, and tables were burnt. Some of the most highly respected citizens leapt into the fire. Then everyone ran to the walls in order to be there before the Carthaginians began to attack again. The fear of poverty and disgrace made death more desirable to us than naked life. We half-grown boys too had weapons in our hands and grasped them as tightly as a man grasps stakes set to fence off a path at the edge of an abyss. Our hands might be deceived,

20

and so might our eyes. The grey monsters, who were now to be seen in the distance approaching the walls, looked like enchanted rocks on which little flames were dancing their devilish dances. They advanced in a ghostly procession. In the end we realized that they were war elephants with bunches of red feathers on their heads. Their drivers were half hidden behind this fearsome red. The sight of these elephants, encased in armour and with saddle-cloths on their backs, paralysed us.

Then the man with the flaming cloak was suddenly to be seen again outside the walls. He called out something to the Carthaginians which they answered with the kind of howl that comes from animals. Then we knew that he had promised them the town as booty.

Many of the townsfolk took flight. I was unable to move and stood there watching the armoured Africans beginning to loosen the walls with crow-bars and heavy hammers. The stones gave way. They had been laid on top of one another without mortar and then simply coated with clay. Close to the place where I was standing the wall cracked and then collapsed. A cloud rose up. When it had dispersed I could see the elephants being driven towards the breach. They were waving their trunks and roaring. The spear I was holding slipped out of my hands.

I jumped down from the wall and ran. Many of the houses were already on fire. I ran through the smoke. I called, 'Father! Mother! Brother!' How I found my way to our house I don't know. Neither do I know what struck me and threw me to the ground. Round about me were walls of fire. Suddenly there was nothing but night.

2

WHEN I came to myself an elephant with only one tusk was standing in front of me. He was so near me that he blocked out half the sky. My eyes travelled slowly up him. On his head was something that astonished me. It was a thick bunch of long reddish rods. It looked to me as if butterflies of the same colour were resting on them. I racked my brains as to what it really could be. I remembered the fearsome red tufts which all the elephants had had on their heads as they advanced towards the walls. They had completely disappeared; when I looked carefully at the elephant's head there was nothing whatever on it. It was bright daylight. I looked for the sun. It must be behind the elephant because it was nowhere else to be seen. Then it had been the sun that had planted the red rods on the elephant's head, just as it sends up clusters of sunbeams over the horizon before it rises—so I said to myself. But why had they suddenly disappeared then? Neither the elephant nor I had moved. It must have been the sharp look I gave the mysterious cluster that had cut it off so suddenly—I could find no other explanation.

The elephant held his enormous head a little to one side. I could see one eye very well. He looked at me calmly out of this, which was no bigger than a horse's eye. He did nothing whatever to frighten me. I was not afraid until the driver looked at me. His face was divided into two pieces by a scar and it made me fear the worst. Then I saw the elephant touch the driver with his one tusk, and I heard the man and the elephant taking counsel together. Then the driver pulled me up out of the rubble. While I was trying to get my balance on my feet the man explained to me that the elephant had interceded for me. 'He has recognized his future driver in you,' he said; 'I am to make a driver of you.' I understood him although he spoke our language very badly. When he talked to the elephant he called him Suru. That was how I knew what the elephant's name was. Finally we rode on him to the camp. I let them do what they liked with me. It was amazing to find myself suddenly on the back of an elephant who had broken down walls. It gave Suru no trouble to climb over the ruins. It was marvellous to me that a giant of that size could move so gently. He planted his feet down as if they had no weight to carry. Without once hesitating he found his way out of the devastated town. Afterwards I noticed the iron hook hanging from the saddle. The driver never needed it. In the camp he showed me to the other drivers. They called him Carthalo. Carthalo told everyone who was willing to listen that it was Suru who had found me. He made them lay me on the ground and then he acted as if he were the elephant. He walked up to me, planted one foot down on my shoulder and then raised it again immediately. He took two steps back, then stood still and turned his head as far round as an elephant can turn it. I let

23

all this be done to me without resisting, and looked across to Suru who was standing not far away, fastened to a stake in the ground, in a line with the other elephants. He didn't seem to pay much attention to what was going on round him. The grey giant swayed a little from side to side, like a ship lying at anchor and moving gently with the swell. It comforted me to see him swaying backwards and forwards. And then I caught myself trying to hold an imaginary conversation with Suru.

Carthalo took hold of me by the shoulder. In the faulty Iberian which the Carthaginians spoke who had lived in our country for a year or two he said, 'Come with me, you belong to us now.'

I stood up and looked him in the face. The scar made me think in a flash: he carries lightning in his face. I was still frightened of him although he had done so much for me. He took me into his tent and showed me my place. He gave me a covering. Then he shared what food he had with me and as he gave me the different kinds of food he said the Carthaginian words for them and told me that I should soon speak as they did.

When I had eaten I felt dead tired. He saw it—he missed nothing. He spread an animal's hide on the floor for me. I fell asleep almost before I had stretched myself out on it. It was about midday when I went to sleep. I don't know how long I slept—the rest of that day and the night, or even two days and nights. The cold woke me up. I must have rolled over in my dreams and thrown my covering off; I must also have cried out because Carthalo felt for me with his hand and covered me up again. I stayed awake and could hear that he had fallen asleep again immediately.

Without making a sound I pushed the covering off, crept on it up to the slit in the tent through which I saw the stars, and then slipped out into the night. I wanted to find out where Suru was. When my eyes had accustomed themselves to the dark I could see the elephants. They stood side by side like a line of hills, but one seemed to me to be smaller than all the others. I began to walk towards them and then remembered the chain with which

24

Carthalo had tethered Suru. I found the path between the tents that led out of the camp. I met no guards. There was no sentry duty—and of what use would it have been, since there was no longer an enemy?

Now that I had the camp behind me I was for a moment in doubt as to where Saguntum was. The darkness was heaped up at a place beneath two stars which were twinkling just above the horizon. I walked in that direction. I wandered about in the ruins, many of which were still smoking. It was beginning to get light when I found the place where our house had once stood; it was now a heap of rubble. I sat down to wait. I was waiting for my father, for my mother, for my brother. I intended to wait until one of them came, or until I was dead.

It was now daybreak and I began to feel cold. The sun rose; it was so pale that it looked as if it were bleeding to death. I watched it and felt astonished that it had the strength to climb up the sky. Just as it was beginning to warm me I saw someone coming. I knew at once who it was but I made no attempt to run away. I couldn't get up. I felt as if I was tethered to the ground.

Carthalo was alone; he hadn't brought Suru. I felt a choking in my throat and thought, Now there's no one there to tell him what to do.

He came up to me, stood still and looked at me, but not angrily. When he began to speak the choking in my throat stopped. He was talking about Suru and nothing else. He said one sentence over and over again: 'Suru is waiting for you.' He was talking Carthaginian, and only now and again put in a word of the language that was foreign to him. But I understood him. When he stopped speaking I plucked up my courage and looked at him. I saw the scar on his face, but now I thought, How can he help his face being cut into two? He certainly didn't do it himself. Someone else had done it to him, someone whom I suddenly and with horror saw before me. It was a man who looked like my father when he seized his weapons. And I had seen the same face many times on other men. At the moment when a

25

man wanted to kill, he lost his own face and took on another out of which Death looked.

Behind Carthalo I saw the ruins which a few days ago had been houses. Carthalo was one of the men who had destroyed Saguntum. He had been sent to kill me but he had not killed me. And now he had come to look for me a second time.

The longer I looked at him the more difficult it was for me to imagine that men like him had laid Saguntum level with the ground. I tried to make myself believe that an earthquake must have destroyed the town, not the man in the red cloak, not men like Carthalo. I wanted to live at peace with this man who came from Suru.

Carthalo sat down beside me. He took a piece of bread out of his pocket and shared it with me. I was hungry and ate. The sun was warm, I was no longer shivering. When we had eaten we sat side by side without speaking.

I noticed that Carthalo was wearing a broad leather strap on his right wrist. The strap was worn and greasy and it shone in the sunlight almost as if it was metal.

Now and again Carthalo looked at me, holding his head a little to one side in a way that reminded me of Suru. The sun did him good. He looked up at it but could not look for long—it was already too strong.

Suddenly Carthalo pointed to a black beam of wood which lay close to our feet. A lizard was peeping out of a crack. It was green and the green stood out sharply against the charred wood. To begin with, only half of it was to be seen; it was a little while before it dared to come right out. Then I saw that it had lost its tail; only a stump was left. The lizard ran a little way very fast, then lifted its head and turned it with a slight jerk. Carthalo was leaning forward; he put his hand invitingly palm upwards on the ground. The lizard was curious and ran a little nearer; perhaps it was fascinated by the shining leather bracelet. It glided on to Carthalo's hand and he shut it quickly. Once again I was frightened. But then Carthalo picked the lizard up between two fingers and pointed to the stump of its tail.

c

'It will grow again,' he said, and let the lizard go. Then he tapped me on the shoulder. 'Suru,' he said, as if to remind me, and then he stood up.

And I went with him.

3

A TIME was coming for the elephants when they could just be elephants.

The war was over. The colder season was at hand, and the soldiers who had asked for leave were sent away to their homes until spring, to Barbary, to the Balearic Islands, to the villages of Iberia either near or far. Only in the forts and watch-towers along the coast were garrisons left. Guards were left behind in the camp, for the most part Numidians and Spartans.

The camp was set up near New Carthage, the capital of the country. This city too was on the sea and had grown up quickly to prosperity. Its harbour was open towards the south, as that of Saguntum had been. Hardly a day passed without ships sailing between the old and the new Carthage. They carried silver, timber, and mercenaries to Africa, and from Africa they brought many kinds of coveted merchandise, from ivory to slaves, and most of this did not stay in the new Carthage but was sold again to traders from other parts of the country. Many of the mercenaries found the town so enchanting that they forgot their homes. The guards too spent most of their free time there, and when they went back to the camp they boasted of what they had seen and done in the town. A good deal of this was not meant for my ears, but mostly they were too drunk to be able to make distinctions. One of the Carthaginians who had been at sea for many years used to go up to the top of the cliff near the harbour and wait for the sunrise, not for the sake of the sun but for the sake of the ships that sailed into the harbour at daybreak. Many arrived with blood-red sails, he said. I had seen the same

28

thing at Saguntum and did not want to see it from the new town.

The elephants gave me enough to do, above all Suru. I had to feed him and keep him clean, as far, that is, as he didn't look after himself. The more familiar I grew with those gigantic animals, the more they astonished me. Everything about them was extraordinary, even their thirst and their hunger. Suru would easily consume about a hundred pounds of food a day, not counting what he sucked up with his trunk. He could easily hold a pailful of water in his trunk; he sucked it up, then raised his trunk and squirted the water into his mouth. He picked up solid food with his trunk too and then shoved it into his mouth. At the same time he was fastidious and left untouched much of the food that I brought him. It sometimes happened that he rejected the branch of a tree for no other reason than that it hadn't been cut off smoothly, or because it had withered leaves still hanging on it. When he himself pulled branches off a tree he wasn't so particular and would overlook splintered ends. He would have preferred to get all his meals without our help, and in this he was the same as the others. They were all greedy: they peeled the bark off trees in order to get to the juicy insides, made furrows with their tusks to expose the roots, tore up clumps of grass and let them fall when they had finished chewing them. Whenever they smelt onions, they knelt down and dug up the soil or poked holes in it with their trunks until the coveted dainties came to light. When the sun was too hot, which was seldom the case now, it sometimes happened that they used the branch of a tree to fan themselves and afterwards ate the leafy parts of it. When they wanted to get the fruit off a tree they shook it with their heads until the fruit fell off, and it was a long time before their patience wore out, but at last, if the tree showed no signs of understanding what was wanted of it, they began to use their tusks like crow-bars, splitting the main root and felling the tree.

Suru had only one tusk, the right-hand one, and I never saw him use it violently. When I pointed this out to Carthalo he said, 'He's only got his beauty tooth, his servant tooth is lost.'

29

The left-hand tusk of the elephants was called the *gumbiro*, a word which means *servant*, because the elephants used it first and foremost for digging and shoving; on the other hand they took care not to damage their *lugori*, or right-hand tusk, so as to be able to present it in an unspoilt condition to the world. At least that's what the drivers said. When Carthalo began to talk about Suru or the other elephants you might just as well expect a full well to run dry as him to stop. He could give me a perfect explanation of why Suru's foot had not crushed my shoulder. 'They have cushions hidden in their feet,' he revealed to me. 'Believe me, there's something in them that you won't find in any other animal. Even I who have lived with them for so long am again and again amazed when I see how easily these gigantic creatures get over obstacles, how gracefully they lie down and stand up.' Carthalo told me more than one elephant's secret. One day he said: 'You can tell by any elephant's foot how tall he is. Twice round his foot gives his height. And do you know how far those great pillars can carry an elephant in one night if he runs away? Almost farther than a horse could go in ten hours. An elephant can depend on his legs. And still more on his ears! He can set them like traps and catch the tiniest sound with them, the cracking of a twig, the rising of a bird.' Carthalo admired the elephant's trunk above all. 'He can hit anything he likes with it,' he assured me. 'You can take it from me. One blow is enough to lay a man flat or to break a lion's backbone. His trunk serves the elephant as nose, as drinking-tube, as weapon, and as hand; he can pick up the smallest coin out of the dust with it if you draw his attention to it. He can pack layers of cool mud on to his own back with it or bore holes for water, and if he feels himself attacked he turns his trunk into a snake raising its neck in fury.' Whenever Carthalo got on to the subject of Suru's trunk he was almost carried away by his enthusiasm. 'Just take a good look at him! He has only one "finger" at the end of his trunk, not two like the other elephants, just as he has only one tusk.' He didn't try to hide the elephant's defects from me. 'There, where the head begins, is a weak spot. No elephant can look

30

round, and besides that their big ears are in their way. It's easy to attack an elephant from behind, and he knows that and therefore never feels quite safe. His neck is his weak spot: he can't shake anyone off it—and so we sit there and have him under control.'

I discovered many things myself through being with the elephants. Not a day passed without my having something to do

for them. At night-time I was so near them that I could feel them standing there in the darkness. There were forty of them. Soon I knew them all by name. And they knew me.

Carthalo was right. From behind they were not to be taken too seriously. Behind, their skin fitted too loosely; there were folds in it which made you think the giant had stopped growing behind before it had finished in front. Only the tail looked dangerous, particularly the end of it, from which bristles stuck out like nails.

Gradually I came to understand what they said. When something pleased them you could hear a murmur coming up out of their throats. If something amused them they made a squeaking sound near the end of their trunks. When they were taking counsel together you could hear a rumbling. They showed fear by a clattering noise deep down in their chests, rage by a roar that made you think the animal would burst. Once when one bull elephant rushed at another he let out such a terrible noise that I turned cold with fright. But as a rule they were on good terms with one another and with their drivers, who were called Indos. Each Indos behaved as if all the other elephants were nothing in comparison with his. Each felt his elephant as part of himself, and woe betide the man who took it into his head to make unfavourable remarks about an elephant; he would pay for it later without a doubt.

The elephants didn't mind cold weather. They felt the heat more than cold, and even now they would occasionally give themselves a dust-bath in the midday hours, particularly if they felt it was time to be rid of the tiresome chains on their feet so that they could trot down to the river, which had a wide ford at this place where it came nearest to the camp. Sometimes they just threw up clouds of dust to make sure what quarter the wind was in.

Dust was very much a second-best: they had a strong urge to get to water. They loved water more than anything. As soon as they got to the river bank many of them walked into deeper places, till all you could see of them was their heads and backs.

32

Others took their time—they dived into the water as gently as a cloud. Then again others made a great splash as if huge pieces of rock had fallen into the water. This was particularly true of the younger elephants; they squirted water at one another and even took it into their heads to wash the rocks which were above water-level. They made balls out of clay and saw who could roll them farthest. They romped together over the balls, or three or four of them would fall upon the Dwarf, an elephant who was fully grown but no bigger than a four-year-old calf elephant. He had no need to be frightened; the bigger ones were only teasing him and never went too far. You could see that they were fond of him. A dark-skinned giant had been chosen to be the Dwarf's Indos, and he towered far above him. 'Who else can say that of himself,' he boasted to the others, 'and which of you has an elephant who is friendly with everybody?' The dark-skinned giant was right; everyone spoiled the Dwarf. But the big elephants were sometimes the victims of petty jealousies or even of persecutions which found vent in kicks or blows with their trunks. Each elephant had his special friends, and lived with the others on more or less friendly terms.

4

Suru's friends were Arba and Tembo. They were considerably taller than he, but when the three stood apart from the others, linked together by their trunks, deep in silent communion, Suru tried not to appear too different from his friends, and even if he didn't quite succeed where his back was concerned, he held his great head in such a way that his eyes were on a level with the eyes of Arba and Tembo.

Suru had also an enemy, Rocco, a bull elephant in his prime. He was younger than Suru, who was over seventy and who already had his fourth teeth, so Carthalo said. It is true that Rocco never dared to attack Suru, but when by chance they met one another you could hear a growling, and it was out of Rocco that the growling came. Suru didn't allow himself to be upset.

But it was not so with Carthalo. It annoyed him when Rocco was in any way offensive to Suru, and sometimes he let his annoyance out on Rocco's driver.

'Why don't you look after that rascal of yours better?' Carthalo called out.

'Why don't you take yours to the slaughterer?' retorted Rocco's driver. His name was Gisgo. And at that point they usually began to let fly at one another like fighting cocks, and Rocco accompanied his driver's abuse with a dull growl, which made Carthalo try to get the same out of Suru. But Suru was not to be moved. Only once did he show his mettle. Gisgo had let himself go so far as to call Suru an old crock, who was past being able to uproot a tree or even to pick up a tree trunk from the ground. At that Suru growled. Perhaps he was irritated by Gisgo's voice which had cracked with rage in his last sentence.

Carthalo was beside himself with fury. At the camp exit there was a pile of tree trunks of different sizes. The whole company of drivers surrounded Suru and Rocco and led them to this pile. It was not the first time that there had been a contest of this kind, but this time the two strongest elephants were facing one another. Some of the heaviest tree trunks were chosen. It was arranged that Rocco should carry the trunks one by one to Suru, and that Suru should carry them back to the pile. The elephants were cheered on by loud shouts. I cheered too when it came to Suru's turn.

Rocco managed all the trunks except the last, which was so heavy that it had needed levers to move it. Rocco struggled with the heavy tree and he was able to raise the thinner end a little way from the ground. His Indos was waving him on with his arms so violently that drops of sweat were breaking out on him.

Rocco tried again and again. But at last he thrust the end of his trunk into his mouth and moved his body so far round that Gisgo could no longer look him in the eyes. The Indos stared at the creased hind-quarters of the elephant towering up in front of

34

him; his foot was already raised to give Rocco a kick, but at the last moment he changed his mind.

Suru was led up. He felt the tree trunk carefully all over. Then he folded his trunk round it and raised it a little to find out whether the balance was right. Finding that it hung down on one side he put it down again. He made this test a second, third, and fourth time, and at last he found the right place and began to walk away with the trunk.

The onlookers were all struck dumb with amazement. There was not a single shout, not even from Carthalo. Suru put down the heavy trunk on the heap.

'Of course he's more experienced,' said Gisgo angrily, to explain Suru's success, and when no one paid any attention to this objection, he cried out, 'And yet he's such a coward that he'll run away from a rat.'

'You're wrong there: he doesn't run away from you,' argued Carthalo.

'He's even frightened of an unsteady log of wood.'

'That we can soon test.'

By now they had almost come to blows again, but as usual their red faces stopped a hand's breadth away from one another. It looked as if they were going to spit at one another. This they did not do—but Rocco's driver spat out a plan for the test. Over one of the ditches which had been dug by the mercenaries when they were making entrenchments outside the camp, six of the tree trunks on which Rocco and Suru had tried their strength were laid. The outer trunks were kept firmly in position by stakes, while the inner ones were laid loosely on wooden blocks, in such a way that they would wobble if anyone stepped on them, not to any great extent but enough to be noticed. The ditch was as deep as a man's height and about five paces wide. Gisgo felt quite confident this time. He led his elephant up to the ditch, walked over the bridge without him and then ordered Rocco to follow him. Rocco didn't hesitate. He walked quickly on to the bridge and so was half across before the trembling beams made him feel uncertain and startled, but he took the two or three steps necessary to reach his Indos who was holding out a whole handful of salt towards him.

Suru had noticed Rocco's hesitation. He was already nervous when Carthalo led him up to the bridge. Carthalo spoke sooth-

ingly to him and then walked over. Then he called Suru. Suru, accustomed to obey, put one foot on the tree trunks and then took a second step. After that he stood still. One of the trunks had moved slightly. Rocco's driver offered Carthalo some salt. Carthalo panted out, 'He'll do it without salt.' But Suru couldn't overcome his fear in spite of all Carthalo's enticements. The elephant took the first two steps again and again, but he didn't get any farther. Carthalo walked towards him; he too took the two steps forward and backward and in his case it looked ridiculous. The onlookers laughed loudly. Then Carthalo stamped his foot, slipped, and fell down. Suru turned round, so frightened that his

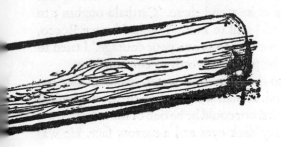

hind legs slipped on to the tree trunks, and when they shook his nervousness made him drop something. It was a cylindrical block with pieces of branch in it, and it was steaming.

The Indos who were watching roared with glee. And so did I. Carthalo had got on to his feet again and he climbed over the steaming pile. He had no eyes for anything but Suru. He shrieked at him as he had never done before: 'Here, come with me!' The whole way back he walked in front raging and stamping. Suru followed three or four paces behind. Now he was holding the end of his trunk in his mouth as Rocco had done. Still in a fury Carthalo tethered him and then disappeared into his tent. He was not to be seen for the whole of the rest of the day.

I stayed with Suru. I talked to him, but I had the feeling that he had shut himself up as he stood there. 'Carthalo oughtn't to have let you in for that,' I said to him. 'You had beaten Rocco, and there was no need for you to prove your courage.' I tried to think what else could be put into words to comfort him.

'It would be better to give him some water,' said someone behind me. I looked round. A man was standing there who looked different from the drivers, nor could he be one of the mercenaries.

He had large and very dark eyes and a narrow face. He was hardly taller than I was.

'I am Silenos, the Secretary,' said the man, who seemed to be about forty years old.

'Do you think that Suru is thirsty?' I asked him.

'Fetch a bucketful, or better still two.'

I fetched water. Suru took a trunk-ful, and then squirted it first on to his legs and chest, then on to his flanks and his back.

'Why does he do that?' I asked in astonishment.

'He feels himself unclean,' said Silenos. 'He is washing his fear away.'

Suru did it thoroughly. I had to go three times for water.

'Now you can talk to him,' said Silenos. 'He can hear better than the Africans.'

'Isn't he an African?'

'Suru is an Indian—didn't you know that?'

Carthalo hadn't told me. Now I understood why Suru was different in many ways from the other elephants. The light grey of his finely pleated skin stood out from the earth-coloured grey of the others, and his topmost point was not his withers but the middle of his back. His ears were smaller and didn't look threatening like shields, but rather like enormous leaves, and just now as I looked at them they were playing in the wind. Above all it was Suru's forehead that distinguished him from the others; it was high and curved and gave him a dignity which the others lacked.

'To get here he must have put the world, as far as we know it, behind him,' said Silenos. 'I know what a long way it is.'

I looked at him questioningly. 'You've been where Suru comes from?'

'Many of us have been there,' said Silenos. 'Since Alexander went that way a hundred years ago Greeks have always felt the desire to follow his example. And where do you come from?'

'From Saguntum.'

Now Silenos was surprised.

'Suru found me in the ruins.' I told him how it had happened.

'So he chose you himself to be his Indos,' Silenos said thoughtfully. He looked at Suru. 'Now he's got his balance again. Look at him! How much more powerful he is than the others. He with his one tusk is their secret lord and master.'

I noticed that Suru was swaying gently from side to side; he was absorbed in himself.

Silenos asked me to go with him to the elephants' ford. I didn't hesitate for a moment. I liked Silenos.

5

WHEN Silenos and I arrived at the elephants' ford it was glistening in the sun, and the rock on which we sat was as warm as if it was alive. Spring was coming. The afternoons were now noticeably longer, and the brown earth was beginning to turn green. Silenos looked out on to the water. It looked as if he had forgotten me and all about the elephants.

'I don't want to say anything against the others,' he said suddenly; 'I think highly of them too.'

'You mean the Africans?' I said, to make sure.

Silenos looked at me thoughtfully. 'Has Carthalo told you that the forest elephants in the neighbourhood of Sala are believed to be divine animals who come down to earth for a hundred years at a time? And that at the new moon they come together to discuss whether the earth is still deserving of elephants?' Silenos noticed how astonished I was at these questions. 'I know,' he went on, 'that Carthalo looks at elephants differently from me. For him the most important question is whether they are strong and useful in war. But there is nothing brutal about them, even if they do look like rocks in the distance. They have finer perceptions than any other animal. Their backs get sore quickly under loads and nothing goes more against their nature than to break down walls or to trample men underfoot.'

'Carthalo wouldn't agree with you,' I interjected.

'Suru isn't a warrior,' said Silenos firmly. 'The African elephants sometimes act as if they were meant to spread terror around them. When their large ears suddenly stick out from their heads like shields, when they toss their trunks up towards the sky, when they stamp their feet so that the earth quakes beneath them—then it is better to keep away from them. As a rule they like to live in peace, and yet again and again men get the idea into their heads that it is right to put drivers on their shoulders, especially in India. Since Alexander came upon war elephants in his march they have been desired by all rulers with armies of their own; they use them as movable fortresses which they set up here and there to strengthen the line. They even established an elephant market on the shores of the Red Sea. The Pharaohs supplied the Carthaginians with war elephants. Only the elephants didn't always do what was expected of them.

40

It is true that they trampled mutineers and enemies to death after having been worked up into a rage beforehand. But on the other hand it has been known to happen that after a breach had been made in the wall of a besieged town an elephant set out to look for his driver who was lying dead on the battlefield, that on his way he trampled down friend and foe alike, and that at last, wounded and despairing, he laid himself down in the breach of the wall in order to put an end to the slaughter. Nikon was the name of this elephant; his name is remembered to this day.'

Silenos was silent again. The sun had moved farther down the sky, but it still gave us enough warmth. 'In India,' Silenos went on in a more lively tone, 'they say that the god Indra rides on the elephant, and Ganesha, the god of Wisdom, is pictured with an elephant's head. The Indians believe that the universe is borne up by eight elephants. Under the roof of the world, in the forests where Suru grew up, there are ravines filled to overflowing with living things. There the flowers of the almond tree are bigger than butterflies. Eagles circle high up above them. Under the giant trees carpets of moss are spread and on moonlit nights yaks and rabbits play on them. And even elephants sometimes dance there, enchanted by the moon, and with the moon they make their way into the jungle, as noiseless as clouds sailing into the darkness of the sky.

'The Indians call the elephant *Hastin*, skilful with the hand. Elephants are great travellers; they are for ever setting out to look for water. They send scouts ahead who report from great distances when they have discovered a feeding-ground. Mountains are not insuperable obstacles for them; they aren't even afraid of snow. They can find a way where there is no road. Suru has made a long journey—it is that that marks him out from the others.' After a pause Silenos added: 'One day he will make his way back again.'

I looked at him in alarm.

'The Indians call it *Mahaprasthan*, the great adventure. No one can escape it.'

Now the elephants' ford had turned red. The sun was low down over the horizon. Silenos looked towards it and his face glowed. 'Let us go back before it gets cold,' he suggested.

I went with him to his tent which was outwardly in no way different from Carthalo's tent.

'I have only been in the camp a few days,' said Silenos. 'I was

42

in Gades—with Hannibal. As soon as the camp fills up with mercenaries he too will come back. If you would like to, come again tomorrow,' he said before he went into his tent.

6

DURING the next few days more and more of the mercenaries who had gone on leave began to arrive at the camp. Some came with donkeys loaded with all that they had been given at home for the journey. 'That will last me till Rome!' I heard one of them boast.

In the camp there was such merry-making that no one needed to go to the town. There were nights when the mercenaries were so riotous that the elephants grew restless. The Indos complained to the captains but the captains only laughed: 'What will it be like when the real thing begins!'

Carthalo found an unfailing way to keep Suru quiet. He tied a live chicken to both the forelegs of the elephant and Suru was so anxious not to tread on the chicken that he didn't move from the spot. Carthalo still bore a grudge against Suru for his 'failure'. He was always arranging tests for him and insisting that others besides me should watch them. Suru accomplished all the tasks that were set him. He carried enormous loads, surmounted obstacles, and stamped holes in the ground where Carthalo demanded it of him so deep that a man could stand up to his knees in them. Carthalo called it trenching. If water collected at the bottom of the hole Suru sucked it up.

'Elephants are expert well-diggers,' said Silenos when I told him about the 'trenching'.

One day, when I had been with Silenos, Carthalo challenged me. 'The best thing would be for you to move over to his tent for always.'

'Am I there too often?' I asked him.

'Yes,' he said rudely. And then what he had been bottling up

D   43 inside him came out. He used the word 'Greek' as a term of abuse. He accused Silenos of having opinions that would make a true Carthaginian see red. He held it particularly against him that a Celt or even a Roman was as much a human being in his eyes as a Carthaginian. 'And a man like that is Hannibal's Secretary,' Carthalo cried indignantly. Then he reproached me for having forgotten who had dug me out of the rubble. I looked at him but said nothing. He asked me to defend myself. I was still silent. Then he softened a little and admitted that I hadn't given Suru any cause for complaint. 'I only don't want you to turn into a Greek,' he said; 'you have the soul of a Carthaginian in you.' Finally he declared, 'There's no ill-feeling between us.' He took a coin out of his pocket and polished it on his sleeve. Then he showed me the side on which was a prancing horse. 'You see his forelegs are raised. Anyone who dared to get in his way would pay for it. Hadad, the war god of the Carthaginians, taught him to rear. You must know that at the place where the Carthaginians planned to build their city they uncovered first the skull of an ox—a certain presage of plague and defeat. That was not at all in accordance with their plan. They began to dig at another place. There they uncovered the skull of a horse, and that promised them dominion over other peoples.' He rubbed the face of the coin until the horse began to sparkle. 'I will give you Hadad's horse,' he said. But he didn't give me the coin; he drew me out of his tent. I had no idea what he had in mind to do, but it seemed important to him that everything should take its proper course, according to his plan.

He untethered Suru. Paying no attention to the stares and questions of the others, he led the elephant and me to a patch of sand half-way between the pile of wood and the ditch which Suru had refused to cross. It was now plain that he wanted to give Suru a chance to make up for his failure.

He gave me a quick look. 'Suru shall give it to you,' he explained. Standing in front of the elephant he threw the coin between Suru's legs, so that it fell down behind him where he couldn't see it.

44

The coin fell into the sand and disappeared without a trace. Suru was given the order to look for the coin. He turned round, stood still for a moment as if he wanted to collect his thoughts, and then began to feel over the sand.

Before long he had fished the coin up out of the sand with his trunk finger and was offering it to Carthalo. Carthalo pointed to me. Suru held it out to me and I took it. I looked at it uncomfortably.

'Don't you want it?' asked Carthalo.

'Yes, I do,' I said, 'but—Hadad's horse isn't on it.'

He took the coin. Instead of the horse there was a palm-tree on it.

'What does this mean?' he cried indignantly. He threw the coin away angrily. Suru saw it fall and, although Carthalo tried to hold him back, he walked to the spot, picked it up, and offered it to me a second time.

'Find Hadad!' Carthalo's order rang out sharply.

Suru obeyed. He searched for so long a time that Carthalo finally lost patience and began to dig in the sand with his own hands. I too joined in the search. Suru watched us. The coin was not to be found.

'He has swallowed it,' said Carthalo furiously. Or had the sand swallowed it up? I held the coin that Suru had given me tightly in my hand. Carthalo was so angry that he never thought of asking me for it. As after the unfortunate test with the wobbling tree trunk, so now: Carthalo stamped furiously along in front of Suru.

In the meanwhile the camp had grown noisier. There was a confusion of shouting among the mercenaries. Soon we could distinguish the words 'Hannibal is coming!'

Carthalo's mood changed suddenly. 'Now everything will be different!' he cried cheerfully. 'No more lounging about! Now all of us will have the chance to show what stuff we're made of— this fellow too!' He gave Suru a friendly poke.

Silenos passed us, also in a hurry. He was going to the open space in the middle of the camp where a red tent was being set up.

45

Carthalo sent a contemptuous look after him. 'That man will never understand what can be done with elephants. But Hannibal knows. You can see for yourself. Even before he arrives things begin to move!' Carthalo walked faster; he had suddenly become as spry as a man ten years younger. I was about to bend down but he was before me; he picked up the chain with which Suru was to be tethered. Then he joined the other drivers. As soon as I was alone with Suru I opened the hand in which I was holding the coin. It was smaller than the one with the horse on it, but I was glad that I had this instead of the other. Suru had given it to me—had given it to me twice in fact. The palm-tree was very faint, but I didn't mind that. I didn't even polish the

coin; I put it just as it was in a little bag which I wore on a
leather cord round my neck. It had held the coins I used to save
in it. Following the lead of all the others I had thrown those
coins into the shaft where the rich men had deposited their
treasures. Now the coin that Suru had given me had the little
bag all to itself.

That evening it was made known in the camp that Hannibal
would arrive in two days. Immediately after his arrival he intended to hold a review of his army; the elephants were to take
up their position at the wings.

'You won't recognize them,' Carthalo declared, and his eyes
shone as if he had a fever.

7

Not only Carthalo—everyone in the camp had caught the fever. Weapons and war materials were feverishly tested and repaired. The mercenaries' faces were red; they held spear-heads and sword blades up in the sunlight to make sure that they gave out enough sparkle. Rust spots were cleaned off armour. The mounted troops scrubbed their horses and polished their saddles and weapons so vigorously that, in the end, from their helmets down to their horses' hoofs all was gleam and sparkle. The camp roads were swept, carpets were unrolled outside the red tent, and large purple flags were hoisted on poles. These flags and the tents themselves waved in the wind that came in from the sea. The air rang with questions, cries, and commands, sometimes also with roars, when one captain fancied that his horse didn't shine as brightly as another's, or if a trace of rust was found on one of the hurling-engines. If a man overlooked a dull patch on his shield he found himself threatened with a worse punishment than if he had committed a murder, and it even happened that companies of a hundred men were ordered by their officers to plough up the sand outside the camp with their knees and elbows, without being given enough time to put the required sparkle on their weapons. The higher a man's position in the camp, the more agitated he was—that was the general rule. The Indos too were so excited that many of them quite lost their heads. Carthalo did what had to be done with calm deliberation; he also lent a hand to several of the others who were afraid of not being ready in time. In any case the Indos had to help one another; one man alone can harness a horse, but not an elephant.

'You won't recognize Suru!' Carthalo announced for the second time, as we led Suru towards the tents in which the elephants' equipment had been stored for the winter.

After a few hours I was standing beside a giant who was hardly recognizable as Suru. A blanket of fearsome scarlet hung down

48

over his flanks; his breast was hidden by an iron plate studded with spikes. On his head a cluster of ostrich feathers had been planted; they were red as though they had been washed in blood. Suru had turned into a fortress which was ready, at Carthalo's command, to set itself in motion.

And that he did in a voice which I didn't recognize as his. The movable fortress took up the position that Carthalo had intended for it. He led him in front of the other drivers so that they might admire him, and he himself praised what the other drivers had made of their elephants.

They were like the elephants that I had seen from the walls ot Saguntum before it was destroyed. Now I could see them near at hand—without the slightest fear. Suru seemed depressed. He looked listlessly out into the distance. I asked Carthalo whether anything was the matter with him.

'What could be the matter with him?' Carthalo retorted. 'He looks much grander now than he ever could just as himself.' He broke off the conversation, annoyed with me or Suru—I wasn't quite sure which.

'Mind you don't disgrace me tomorrow!' he charged Suru. 'He'll look at you more closely than at any of the others. He counts on you, you know.' It was impossible to know whether Suru had taken in what Carthalo had said to him. And that evening when he was tethered to his post, without his scarlet covering, his breast-plate, and his tuft of feathers, he stood there silent and remote. It was the same with the other elephants. They all looked sullen. It was clear that they didn't like what was being done to them.

Carthalo turned away from him. On his way to the tent he said nothing, but inside the tent he gave vent to his annoyance.

'What makes him take it into his head to stand there like the inoffensive grass-eater that he once was, instead of like the giant he is, who can make legions tremble?'

Carthalo was angry; he looked as if he would like to rush at someone, but this time in earnest, not as when he let fly at Rocco's driver. His eyes had an unkind gleam in them, his scar was throbbing. 'That breed of wolves!' he said, in a voice full of hatred. 'What are elephants for but to trample them to death!' His face took on its usual expression again; only his eyes still looked angry. 'It's not a simple matter, first to catch them and then to train them so that they are fit for war,' he said. 'In Barbary there are forests and ravines in which they know their way about better than we do. On the steppe they even post sentries, sharp fellows who keep a damned good look-out for anything dangerous that might be in the wind. They often play us a trick and escape, but sometimes the wind is against them, that is, when it blows from them and not towards them. Then it may happen that they fall into the traps which have been prepared and covered over a long time ago. They are quite unsuspicious. Suddenly there is fire behind them and all round them. It is not the steppe that is on fire—it is the torches that the drivers are waving. The herd is beginning to panic, everything around them throws them into confusion. They follow their leader and run wherever he runs. He has noticed a gap in the circle of fire. At the gap are the ditches which have been dug to trap them. If they fall into these ditches they no longer belong to the herd but to us. At first they can't believe that we are their friends. Hunger helps them to understand. After a few days, when they begin to take food out of our hands, they change into different creatures. A little piece of us goes into them. Then they are brought to Carthage. In the inner wall of the city there are stables for three hundred elephants. They go through the wall into the city and become Carthaginians—just as you have become one.' He looked at me more closely. 'Lord of the World!' he cried. 'I've been so busy with the elephant that I've forgotten all about you. You can't go before him looking like that.'

Carthalo was dressed in the purple tunic that all Indos wear when the elephants are in battle array. I was still wearing the clothes I had worn in Saguntum. Now he brought out another purple tunic and insisted that I should put it on. It didn't fit me; it was much too big. 'It doesn't matter,' he laughed, 'you must just hurry up and grow.' He wound a white cloth round my forehead like the one he was wearing. Then he stepped back a few paces and examined me. 'Another Carthalo!' he cried joyfully. 'Suru will be surprised!'

I looked uncomfortably down at myself.

'Look at me!' cried Carthalo, now in a cheerful mood. 'Then you will know what you look like.' I had never seen him so carefree. His gaiety infected me.

'Imagine what a fine figure you will cut on Suru's back tomorrow. I would like to lay a wager that he will speak to you. And I can foretell something else as well: that he will take you for a Carthaginian.' Carthalo stopped suddenly. 'Have you ever seen him?'

'Only his cloak.' I looked down at the ground.

For a moment he was confused. 'Forget it,' he said; 'you see I had already forgotten that you come from Saguntum. And you will forget it too when you see him properly for the first time.'

8

LONG before daybreak Carthalo was up. The sun had not yet risen when he woke me. He had already given Suru water and food. I put on the driver's tunic. We ate hurriedly and after that nothing was important except Suru.

Three hours before midday mercenaries and elephants were drawn up in battle array on the flat ground between the camp and the river. For two more hours commands rang out. Then it was quiet. Signals announced that Hannibal was coming.

I was on Suru's back—between Carthalo and the scarlet feathers. Over the top of the feathers I saw a cloud moving up the river. In the cloud there was a red patch, like the sun before it breaks through the mist. I could see men on horseback drawing rapidly nearer. I could count them; there were eight—besides him. Carthalo whispered to me who the riders were: his brothers Mago and Hasdrubal, Maharbal, commander of the

52

horse, Monomach, leader of the mercenaries, Synhal, his personal physician, Bogu his camp priest—and two extras, Myrkan and Barmokar, two Carthaginian security men. The rest of what Carthalo was telling me was drowned in the uproar of shouting that arose when Hannibal entered the open square formed by the mercenaries, the horsemen, and the elephants.

His escort fell back. Hannibal brought his horse to a standstill. Its black coat shone in flashes and the scarlet cloak of its rider showed up its brilliance. It was a patch of night in the midst of the day, and it outshone the day.

Hannibal raised an arm. There was silence.

Hannibal spoke, first in Carthaginian, then in the languages of the mercenaries. His massed audience gave him an uproarious response. It was as if a magician were calling to one mountain after another, and as if one mountain after another were to awake and set up a roar. Whatever he might call out to the mercenaries was transformed by them into wild acclamation.

Carthalo roared in a frenzy of enthusiasm, and I shouted with him. I shouted even when I didn't understand what Hannibal was saying.

When Hannibal had finished speaking he rode along the front line. He began at the opposite wing to ours, and there were elephants there also. He stopped longer with them than with the companies of mercenaries. Carthalo was afraid that I hadn't understood some of the Carthaginian words that Hannibal had used, and he began to translate his speech into Iberian for me.

He spoke excitedly; his breath pounded at my ear.

'What you have before you now,' he began in a hoarse voice, 'is the best army that has ever marched over this earth. It will shatter Rome to fragments. Rome must not exist any longer. It must no longer be able to fall upon us, as it has already fallen upon a hundred cities. What was Rome to begin with? A muddy village. What were the Romans? Hard-boned peasants who didn't even know how to take hold of an oar. But at that time the seas already belonged to Carthage. Carthaginians were at home on every coast. If Carthage didn't give permission, no

Roman could wash his hands in the sea. And so it shall be again. Barca, the Lightning, gave Carthage a wall that can advance against its enemies: a tried and trusty army, tried and trusty elephants. This wall set itself in motion when Barca sailed across the sea to Iberia to build a new Carthage. Rome has no longer any need to fear the old Carthage. The men there are sitting on red couches; they prefer parleying with Rome to fighting it. Carthage is here!' Carthalo was shouting. 'He is Carthage!' He had to shout to make himself heard, because a company of mercenaries who had just been addressed by Hannibal were answering with shouts of applause. Hannibal was coming nearer. 'I have seen how he deals with his enemies, even when he is outnumbered by them,' Carthalo went on, once more in a lowered voice. 'When the Olcadians wanted to cross the Ebro he let them cross it. He made his army fall back. The Olcadians were drunk with a victory they hadn't yet won. While they were still in the river but already close to the bank where we were standing, Hannibal began to advance against them, with his horsemen and elephants. The Olcadians were standing up to their necks in water, and he let them drown on the point of victory. He knows how to defeat the enemy when they are three to one against us. You can stake your life on him.' Carthalo was shouting again because another company was shouting. 'He thinks for us. If we only hate the Romans as he hates them—it is enough. We will wipe that pack of wolves off the face of the earth. You must hate the Romans because they deserve hatred. They were murderers from the beginning. Romulus, the first Roman, killed his brother Remus, only because he jumped over the ditch that Romulus had dug to make a boundary line between "Yours" and "Mine". Throughout its history Rome has drawn boundary lines that have cost other people their lives. But now Hannibal will cross them.' Hannibal was riding towards the mercenaries who were lined up next to the elephants. Carthalo was leaning so far forward that I could feel his lips touching my ear. 'Now he's coming to you,' he whispered. 'Listen to what I'm going to tell you! He was not even as old as you are now when his father made him

54

swear on the altar of Moloch to hate the Romans. He was only nine years old. You are twelve. Swear!' Carthalo yelled, so that I might hear him through the roars of the mercenaries next to us. 'Swear the oath of Hannibal: I will hate Rome until there is no longer a Rome to hate. I will trample the Romans to death——' He shook me and tried to shout louder than the mercenaries, but I couldn't hear him; the mercenaries were making too much noise.

Now Hannibal was coming towards us. He rode in front of the elephants. When he came to Suru he halted his horse and dismounted. I was amazed to see how little he was. In the saddle he had looked tall; now the horse towered far above him. I saw him open one of the saddle-bags and put his hand into it. He walked up to Suru, holding a lump of salt in his hand. I could see his face now and his eyes, and forgot that he was a little man.

'Suru,' he said, 'old fellow! We haven't seen each other for a long time. How are you?' He held out the salt to Suru and Suru took it.

'We have a long march before us,' Hannibal confided to the elephant, 'on a road that no elephants have yet trod. We are going to climb over the Alps.'

Suru had put the lump of salt into his mouth. His trunk began to swing—a sign that he was happy.

'It won't be a salt-licking expedition,' Hannibal assured him. 'But so far you have done everything that was asked of you.'

Suru put his trunk on Hannibal's shoulder. That he only did to Carthalo and me.

'We understand one another, you rascal!' Hannibal took the trunk and rubbed his cheek on it. Then he looked up at Carthalo and me. 'What's this?' he cried merrily. 'Have you got a son?'

'One might say so,' Carthalo boasted. 'The boy owes his life to me.'

'Well, little Carthalo, how do you get on with Suru?' Hannibal asked.

'It couldn't be better,' I answered in the Carthaginian language.

55

'You aren't a Carthaginian?' Hannibal asked in surprise.

'He's in the middle of becoming one,' Carthalo assured him.

Hannibal laughed. 'You and Suru—you suit one another well.' He was looking at me, not at Carthalo. Never before had I seen such eyes.

'I shall depend on you, you little Carthaginian,' he said to me. 'I can make good use of you and your like.'

My cheeks began to burn. I still felt Hannibal's eyes on me when he had already mounted his horse and was preparing to ride on.

'You will go with him,' Carthalo whispered behind me. 'Do you still want to change places with someone who is not one of us?'

I said no, but the 'no' stuck in my throat.

'Don't forget that you have sworn to hate the Romans as he hates them!'

My eyes were fixed on Hannibal as he rode away. I couldn't bring myself to confess that I hadn't sworn that oath, not even to myself.

9

I SAW him often now, almost every day, and he always noticed me when I came anywhere near him. 'My little Carthaginian,' he cried to me from the distance. He seemed to know everyone in the camp, although there were many thousands, at least forty thousand. He managed to make everyone believe that Hannibal knew him. And perhaps he really did know each man personally. They had all been with him on several campaigns, had shared the spoils of victory with him and never to their disadvantage. They had gone hungry with him, had distinguished themselves, or been wounded, in his presence. Most of them had served under his father and had never had to wait for their pay. Some of them had been rescued from a skirmish by Hannibal himself. They had

lain with him like dead men on fields stained with blood, when after their gruesome labours their weapons had at last dropped from their hands.

I heard all this from Carthalo who, when he had once begun on this subject, could never stop. Since Hannibal had been in the camp he had stopped talking about the elephants and instead had talked almost only of him. 'He is a brother to us all,' he declared, 'just as Barca, his father, was a father to each one of us. It doesn't matter where a man was born—in Hannibal's camp he forgets it and becomes a Carthaginian.'

Carthalo could tell stories about Barca as well as about Hannibal. 'Even when they had driven him into a corner he knew how to turn it to his enemy's disadvantage,' he said. 'Once, when Roman galleys had surrounded Barca's ship with its purple sails, and when the last spears had been thrown, he used earthenware pots as his weapons of defence. He ordered them to be thrown into the ships that were pursuing him. The Romans laughed at the strange missiles, but when the pots broke they stopped laughing. Suddenly their ships were swarming with vipers and these vipers were attacking them viciously. Barca escaped. He escaped also from Erys and Eirkte, the mountain strongholds in which he and his faithful followers had taken refuge during the first war with the Romans. He paid the sum demanded by Rome for honourable withdrawal: eighteen dinars for each man—and Rome, not he, paid the interest, for with these men whose freedom had been bought Barca conquered Iberia, and with them Hannibal will enter Rome, as he promised in Gades.'

Now I knew why Hannibal had been in Gades—the place where Africa and Iberia come nearest to one another, the Pillars of Hercules. He had been persuaded by Bogu, his head priest, to make a sacrifice to this hero who had turned into a god.

'Bogu is always careful to propitiate the gods at due intervals,' said Carthalo. 'In my opinion it's not necessary for a man like Hannibal. Has he not got us? In the whole camp there is no one who would not let himself be torn into little pieces for him—except the two spies,' he corrected himself.

Five days later the names of these two were on everyone's lips.

'Myrkan, Barmokar! Puppets of Rome!' The cry went up from every lane in the camp. The whole camp was in an uproar. Carthalo made me go with him; his eyes had once again a threatening light in them.

'They are in the pillory!' was the cry we now heard.

Everyone was pressing towards a hill outside the camp gate; when we arrived there the hill was already surrounded by a human wall. Carthalo pushed me in front of him. I made my way through the crowd and there were the spies in front of me.

They were shaved bald and their faces bore the marks of the whip—I could hardly recognize them.

Monomach was standing in front of them with a whip in his hand. A Carthaginian I had never seen before was standing beside him.

Monomach, who was in charge of the foot troops, was more feared than anyone else in the camp. He was the idol of the mercenaries and it was said that he had slain more than four hundred enemies with his own hand.

Now, by looking all round him at the human wall, he reduced it to silence. He called upon the unknown man to speak.

The man began to make his statement: 'I come from Carthage. Four days ago ambassadors from Rome suddenly appeared in the city. That we could not object to. They brought a charge against us on account of Saguntum. That also was within their rights. They demanded that Hannibal should be brought to judgement. There was nothing in that to surprise us—we are used to the Romans opening their mouths much wider than becomes them. But now listen to what Hanno, Barca's old adversary, demanded! He, the spokesman of those Carthaginians who choose rather to put their hands in their purses than to take up a weapon, made the proposal that Hannibal should be delivered up to Rome.'

Cries of rage rose up round the hill and met at the top in a wild crash.

'One of Hanno's party even demanded that Hannibal should be treated like a general who has lost a battle, and be crucified.'

Once again the indignation of the listeners found vent in a wild roar.

Monomach gave the two men at the whipping-post a lash with his whip.

'Give it to them!' the wall roared. 'Tear the masks from their faces!'

'They are unmasked,' declared Monomach with a malicious grin. 'We have found out what they have under their coats. The stain from their innermost being has worked out to their skin.'

He tore their coats open. Both men had been branded with the bundle of rods and the axe, the symbol of Rome.

'Traitors!' The roar went up. 'Roman puppets! Scoundrels!'

'Make way for Hannibal!' Monomach cried suddenly.

The wall opened. Through the gap came Hannibal, accompanied by Maharbal and Silenos.

'What's wrong with you?' Hannibal asked the two men in the pillory. 'I hardly know you.'

'Now they are showing us their real faces,' Monomach assured him.

Hannibal walked up to the pillory. Barmokar turned away, but Myrkan stared straight at Hannibal.

'Why do you look at me like this?' Hannibal asked him.

'Because I hate you.'

'And why do you hate me so much?'

'Because I love Carthage.'

'I love Carthage too,' declared Hannibal.

'No!' Myrkan yelled. 'If you loved Carthage you wouldn't destroy it.'

'How can you say that?' Hannibal asked calmly.

'You are like your father!' Myrkan cried. 'He too thought of nothing but war. But your wars will devour more men than his. The ruins of Saguntum will not fall on Rome—they will fall on Carthage.' Myrkan yelled so violently that the weals on his face began to bleed. Hannibal saw the bundle of rods. Taken aback he turned to Monomach. 'You go too far,' he said.

The leader of the mercenaries defended himself. 'Men like that must be branded like cattle, so that there is no doubt where they belong.'

Hannibal gave the order to untie Myrkan.

'Are we to let him go?' Monomach protested.

'Let both go!' The order rang out more sharply.

Both men were untied from the posts.

'Go back to Hanno,' Hannibal charged them. 'Tell him that I am going to do what he suggests: I am going to Rome of my own free will.'

There was an uncanny silence. The onlookers all craned their necks.

'I shall present myself to the Romans,' Hannibal went on, in a tone that banished all doubt. 'These men here will soon all be standing before the gates of Rome.'

Wild applause interrupted him. When the noise had died down he went on: 'It is true that we shall not go as negotiators but as men of action. The Romans won't find us quite so easy to deal with as those Carthaginians who think that everything is to be bought, including offices and dignities. How many pounds did Hanno pay for the post he now holds?' he asked bitingly. 'Fifty, wasn't it?'

Myrkan did not answer.

'Well, his reckoning is right,' Hannibal went on; 'for, according to what one hears, he asked for a hundred pounds from the Romans in return for his offer to deliver me over to them.'

'That is a lie!' cried Myrkan. His protest was drowned in shouts of hatred. Hannibal silenced the crowd. 'Give his parrot our greetings!' he cried to the two men.

Everyone in the camp knew that Hanno's followers had given their leader a parrot who could say 'Hanno is always right'. 'I understand that a parrot will repeat the words he has been taught,' Hannibal went on sarcastically, 'but it surprises me that

61

Hanno can't find anything better to say than what the Romans put into his mouth. Give Hanno the parrot my greetings!'

Waves of laughter followed the two men as they turned away. Beside himself with delight, Carthalo drummed on my back with his fists. He didn't realize that he was hurting me. I couldn't join in the laughter. My eyes fell upon Silenos but his face did not betray his thoughts. When the laughter had subsided, Hannibal turned to the messenger from Carthage. 'What happened then to the Romans in the Council of the Hundred?'

The messenger said, 'When the empty speeches had come to an end our men asked what the Romans wanted now, since they would not get Hannibal. And the spokesman for the Romans put both his hands into his toga and said that he was holding war in one of its folds and peace in the other. "Make your own choice!" our men demanded. Then the Roman opened his right hand and cried, "Then you shall have war!"'

'Do you hear that? War!' Hannibal pronounced. 'They shall have it!'

'War!' roared the thousands of listeners who were making a ring round the hill. The men in front rushed at Hannibal and lifted him on to their shoulders. I lost Carthalo in the crowd. Hannibal was carried down the hill towards the camp. Out of the human torrent that followed him surged the cry, 'Hannibal is right!'

10

SILENOS and I were left behind on the hill. We were standing beside the bare whipping-posts. Silenos was pale. Without saying a word he led the way to the elephants' ford. There we sat down where we had sat the first time. My mind was in a whirl. I couldn't believe that Hanno, a Carthaginian, could have demanded the surrender of Hannibal. Silenos confirmed the fact, but he said not a word against Hanno. He defended him. 'Hanno

62

could not act in any other way. He is a man of the old stock. The Phoenicians, from whom the Carthaginians are descended, were from the beginning good traders, not warriors. They were not interested in the conquest of land—they sailed the seas. They were called the Red Men because the chief article of their trade was purple dye. When the swarm from the Purple Land settled in Africa in order to lay the foundations of Carthage, they paid for the land they needed to build a town and a harbour. Wherever they went they paid: for tin and silver, for gold dust and ivory, for lion-skins and different kinds of woods. So they were always welcome. They paid for everything; that was their way of conquering. They set the stream of goods flowing: amber from the north in exchange for gold from the south, incense from the east in exchange for ships' cables from the west. Everyone profited, they, of course, most of all, but they did good service for their pay. Their ships ventured right up to the islands outside the Gates of Hercules. They even visited that mysterious country Agisymba, where the hippopotami herd. One Carthaginian whose name was Mago crossed the great desert three times, undeterred by sandstorms or by the brigands who lay in wait for travellers at the oases. Others penetrated into those latitudes where the seas freeze over in winter, and one actually sailed with his crew round Africa, and that they actually achieved the undreamed-of is proved by the very thing that is most difficult to believe in their report: the sun, which day after day had risen to the left of them, rose one day on their right hand. They had circumnavigated Africa. Throughout their history Carthaginians have been seafarers, discoverers, desert travellers, traders—but not soldiers. Whenever it was necessary to defend themselves they hired mercenaries. But they hated war. They tried to finish their wars as quickly as possible. If their generals made mistakes they were punished severely. It is true that they crucified their generals who lost a battle.'

'And you think that was a good thing?'

It was not I who asked this question. A shadow fell between Silenos and me. Carthalo was standing behind us.

'I've been looking for you everywhere,' he said reproachfully.
'Sit down here with us!' Silenos urged him. 'We are talking about Carthage.'

'What you've just said is enough for me,' Carthalo said aggressively.

'I hadn't finished,' said Silenos calmly.

'I only want you to tell me one thing,' said Carthalo. 'Supposing it had been you who had had to give the Romans their answer—would you have chosen war?'

'No,' said Silenos. He stood up.

Carthalo walked threateningly towards him. 'Are you a Roman?'

'Should I be here if I were a Roman?' asked Silenos, showing no signs of agitation.

'One never knows with you how long you will be on our side,' Carthalo grumbled.

'You forget who made me his Secretary,' Silenos retorted.

Then Carthalo gave way a little. 'You aren't a traitor,' he said; 'one can tell that by looking at you. But you think too much, and that makes you different from the rest of us.'

'That is possible,' said Silenos.

On the way to the camp he made one or two attempts to get into conversation with Carthalo, but Carthalo seemed to have withdrawn behind a barrier. In the tent, however, he talked to me till late into the night: about the war and the Romans, about the Romans and the war. 'Ask your Greek friend to tell you what Rome is capable of,' he said relentlessly. 'Ask him whether Rome made a pact with robbers to fall on us in Sicily from behind. Ask him whether Rome took Sardinia from us when our hands were tied—during the mutiny of the mercenaries after the first war we had lost! Ask him whether Rome raised the tribute in the times of peace in order to suffocate Carthage with its debts! If Barca hadn't trampled the mutineers to death with elephants in the gorges of the Atlas Mountains, and if he hadn't made Iberia with its silver mines into a new Carthage, we should have suffocated under our load of debts, as Rome had intended.

64

Now Rome is going to be paid back for what it did to us. In the end it will be as it once was: no Roman will be able to wash his hands in the sea unless we allow it. The Romans began the war—we didn't,' he asserted, and he named town after town that had been destroyed by the Romans. Suddenly he stopped short. 'You are thinking of Saguntum,' he said, looking at me searchingly.

'Yes,' I said.

'It was destroyed by Rome,' said Carthalo without hesitating. I looked at him in amazement. Now he stopped talking excitedly. 'You're thinking of the red cloak,' he went on quietly. 'You're thinking of the rams and scorpions and elephants who battered down the walls of Saguntum.'

'But it was Carthaginians who besieged and destroyed Saguntum,' I protested in bewilderment.

'But what had happened before?' Carthalo asked me. 'What about the men who because they had taken Carthage's part were thrown down from the walls of Saguntum?'

I knew that that had happened and didn't contradict him.

'And how had it come to that?' Carthalo then asked.

'I don't know,' I said.

'I will tell you,' he went on in a tone that made me pay attention. 'Rome had stirred up feeling in Saguntum against us. Rome intended that something should take place there that would force Hannibal to attack Saguntum. Rome had only made a treaty with Saguntum in order to goad New Carthage to fury. Rome carried it to such a pitch that Saguntum became a thorn in Hannibal's side. Can he be blamed for pulling it out? And when he did pull it out, did Rome lift a finger to save Saguntum? Rome looked on from the distance while Saguntum perished. Saguntum had played the part that Rome had intended for it—and Rome let it fall.'

He is right, I thought, taken aback. Not a single Roman was there to help us. It wasn't a Roman who pulled me out of the rubble. It was Carthalo, a Carthaginian. It was Carthaginians who took care of me when I was all alone in the world. It was Hannibal's elephant who saved my life.

'Rome betrayed you.' Carthalo said it as if he were pronouncing judgement.

Then he leaned over towards me. 'My little Carthaginian! Hannibal will take vengeance upon Rome for Saguntum.' Then

66

he prepared my bed for me, as he had prepared it on the day when he had rescued me from the ruins of Saguntum. After Carthalo had put out the lamp I lay for a long time with my eyes open and stared into the darkness above me in the tent. I could see Hannibal standing in front of me; his red cloak had no longer any terror for me.

II

DURING the next few weeks the first and last things to be attended to were the army's weapons. I was almost always roused from sleep by the clatter of horses' hoofs, the jingling of harness, and shouted orders, and Carthalo was always awake before me; he laughed at me when he saw that it took me a little time to get used to the day which was still half night. 'You have to crack sleep—like a nut!' he said. He gave such a mighty yawn that his jaws cracked. He enjoyed the life that Hannibal had brought with him. 'Our weapons are sharp,' he assured me; 'now the men are being sharpened, and then we can be off!' Carthalo took me out to the field between the camp and the river where the mercenaries were being drilled. 'They're gradually getting to know which way the wind is blowing—What do you say to those?' He held out the arm on which he wore the leather bracelet, towards a cloud of dust. There were men in the cloud, but I saw only horns and the heads of wild animals with gaping jaws. They were helmets made to terrify the enemy, worn by half-naked men. They rushed at one another howling. 'Our Berserks!' Carthalo said proudly. 'Our Celts! They fight like animals. Death is on their side because they don't fear him.'

Although the mercenaries were fighting with sheathed weapons, I noticed when the dust cloud dispersed that several of them were being carried off the field. I even saw bloodstains. 'Bloodshed belongs to the trade and is part of the training,' said Carthalo with a grim look on his face.

67

The whole field could be seen from the top of a hill. On certain days it was given up to the horsemen. The troops could alter the direction of their charge like lightning, like migrant birds when they change the direction of their flights. Each horseman was followed by a little cloud of dust, and when Maharbal took his place at the head of the six thousand, the clouds turned into a wall which moved across the field and which looked ghostly on windless days. The wall suddenly split into two; the troops surrounded the imaginary enemy with breath-taking speed and deluged them with a ringing hail of short spear-heads that looked like little lightning flashes. The earth thundered under the beat of twenty-four thousand hoofs.

At first this rainless thunder-storm struck me as uncanny, but soon I found myself waiting impatiently for the days when the horse troops took the field.

The elephants too were gradually being trained to the idea that they were there to help in the war. They advanced out of the camp under heavy armour, waiting for orders, and were continually confronted with obstacles which they had to trample down. One day they had to advance against a wood which was occupied by mercenaries. The mercenaries excited them by noisy cries. As in all the exercises in which Suru took part, I was sitting in front of Carthalo, strapped on to the large saddle. Carthalo leant forward and shouted the Great Call into Suru's ear, the cry of a beast of prey that rouses an elephant to uncontrollable fury. The other Indos also excited their animals till they were beside themselves with rage, and the elephants plunged into the wood which had by now been evacuated by the mercenaries. They stopped at each tree. One trunk after another fell with a loud crack. Each elephant trampled a lane clear for himself. The trees crushed the undergrowth as they fell. Carthalo and I ducked our heads under the shields which we carried, but we were in no danger, because the trees were falling in the direction in which we were going and as they fell they brought down with them what might have hindered us in our advance.

'That's what the Romans are in for!' shouted Carthalo, and I shouted too, because I was sitting on an animal who knocked down trees.

In the open field behind the wood the grey avalanche came to a halt. The elephants quietened down because there were no more obstacles confronting them. We looked back. The little wood which had just now been there didn't exist any longer. 'We shall plough up Rome like that,' Carthalo assured me, and I believed him.

He considered that day to mark the end of my education as a driver. He had taught me all the orders and attentions that Suru was used to with the utmost devotion, as if it was his intention to make himself unnecessary. Suru understood twenty-two different words of command. I had learnt these words easily, and it was not long before Suru was able to understand what I meant by them. It was not so easy to master the signs we had to give with our feet, or by the shifting of our weight. I weighed half as much as Carthalo and my legs were not as long as his. But in the end, even with me Suru knelt down when I leaned forward, stood up when I leaned back and went in the direction which I indicated by leaning over to one side or the other. He picked up a stone when I said the Carthaginian word for stone, and my stick when I dropped it, and always during the stick-lifting practice, when it came to the third time, he scratched his flank with it before he gave it back to me, and that meant he had had enough stick-lifting and I must let him off any more. We understood one another without many words. As time went on I even began to flatter myself that Suru liked carrying me better than Carthalo. In any case he never gave me any trouble, whereas with Carthalo he tried every now and again to go his own way, although he never succeeded. Actually, although they all had the same training, each elephant kept his special peculiarities, and it would have been unwise to ignore them.

Some elephants were irritated if you approached them from the right instead of from the left, and Tembo would never let his Indos mount him if he had not first sat down on the ground.

69

All these things were reckoned with; every Indos knew all the elephants, and the mercenaries had strict orders to leave the grey giants in peace.

Now everything began to indicate that the sham fighting would soon be done with and that the march on Rome was about to begin in all seriousness. Every day larger sections of the army were called up for general exercises, and at last the day came when Hannibal paraded all his forces.

That was also the day when Suru carried Hannibal and me for the first time. Hannibal had asked Carthalo whether I was able to drive Suru, and Carthalo had been burning to show what he had made of me.

There was hardly any driving for me to do. After Suru had carried us both to the top of the hill from which the whole field could be seen, Hannibal was in control. At his command the hurlers moved to the attack; at a sign from him the heavy armoured troops were set in motion. He gave the signal that let loose the horse troops in their wedge formation; he brought them back after the engagement and combined them into gigantic pincers—and he did all this without moving from the spot. Horsemen galloped away with his orders and when they arrived at their destination it could be seen that these orders were breaking down any resistance. Hannibal didn't shout or rebuke anyone harshly; he didn't even make Suru nervous, as Carthalo almost always did when he sat on Suru's back and played the commander.

'Suru has never been so quiet,' Hannibal reported when we were riding back to the camp. He said it as if the credit was mine, although I had done nothing whatever to deserve it. Hannibal was satisfied with his mercenaries and horsemen; he praised those we passed on the way to the camp, and the horsemen and mercenaries answered with loud cries and waved their weapons.

'We suit each other well, we three,' Hannibal said to me when we had dismounted. He rubbed his face against Suru's trunk and patted me on the shoulder. Carthalo watched us, full of pride. On that same day the date of the great decampment was settled: it was to be four days later. Six thousand horsemen,

72

thirty-four thousand foot soldiers and all the forty elephants were to go with Hannibal over the Alps.

During the four days before we were to break camp the reins were slackened, for the men as well as the animals. The horses were put out to pasture day and night; the elephants spent half the days at their ford. The mercenaries had unlimited leave and many of them didn't come back from the town till the morning; in the camp also there was drinking and merry-making till far into the night. On the last day a column of wagons rumbled through the camp gateway; they were loaded with jugs and skins full of wine. The merchants of New Carthage were sending the mercenaries a farewell present.

It was good wine. None of the mercenaries thought of leaving the camp. A general banquet began as early as midday. By the evening very few of the men knew what they were doing. They were bawling songs and playing for such high stakes that several had played away a whole year's pay in advance. There were even some who staked their share of the loot in the coming campaign. The wine drove them into madcap escapades: one ran amok and tried to lift an elephant from the ground; he barely escaped with his life from the outraged giant. One captain ordered his company to move out of camp in battle order but without weapons and then to make an assault on the camp at four places; they made wide breaches in the camp palisade.

When darkness began to fall many of the men were lying senseless in their tents or even out in the open, and by midnight all had fallen into a leaden sleep—even the sentinels. Hannibal, who didn't wish to deprive anyone of the merry-making, had ordered them to be relieved at midday.

In Carthalo's tent it smelt of wine as it did in all the others. Carthalo had invited the drivers of Arba and Tembo to be his guests, and he kept on urging me also to drink more: 'Drink! you're a man now! Drink! you trampler-down of Romans! You are riding Suru, Hannibal's elephant!' And I had drunk until there was a red mist all round me. I hadn't even noticed that the two other drivers had gone away.

12

SOMEONE was shaking me. It was someone who had a lantern in his hand. I could see a face and gradually I realized that it was Ittibal, driver of Arba, the she-elephant who was Suru's friend. Ittibal was trying to wake Carthalo too, but Carthalo had drunk more than I had.

'Must it be so early?' I asked Ittibal. 'It's not even light yet.'

Ittibal was quite beside himself and could only talk nonsense. At last I understood: Arba had disappeared. At that I jumped up, fetched a jug of water and poured it over Carthalo's face.

Carthalo started up with a curse. It was some time before he understood what I was telling him.

'Arba gone?' He looked at Ittibal as if he was a ghost.

Ittibal pushed him out of the tent. Outside it was still dark. Sleeping men were lying across our paths and in spite of the lantern we nearly fell over several of them.

'However could Arba have got away—over all these?' Ittibal lamented. 'Elephants,' grumbled Carthalo—it sounded as if he were blaming Ittibal—'How can you be surprised at anything they do!'

When Carthalo came to the peg from which Arba had broken away, he too was bewildered. Again and again he examined the few links of the chain which still hung on the peg. Arba had broken a new chain.

'The elephant must have had an irresistible urge,' he said at last. He threw the light of the lantern on to Ittibal's face and said in a voice full of meaning: 'Don't you think that she's grown very much bigger during the year?'

'She's a good feeder,' Ittibal conceded; 'she ate enough for two elephants.'

'We'll take Suru out and ride after her on him,' said Carthalo grimly. 'If anyone can, he'll be able to throw light on the mystery.'

74

Carthalo insisted that Ittibal should report the matter without delay. 'Hannibal will swallow me whole!' Ittibal lamented. 'In a few hours we march, and my elephant is missing!'

'He'll kill you if you don't report it,' Carthalo assured him. 'You know how important every elephant is to him.'

I saw that Ittibal was trembling. Then I offered to go to Hannibal myself. Much relieved, Ittibal gave me his lantern and I ran off.

Hannibal's tent was no more closely guarded than the other tents. The tent door was open; I walked in and saw by the light of the lantern that, besides Hannibal, Maharbal and Monomach were sleeping in the tent. Hannibal woke up without my having to rouse him, and when he asked what I wanted, Maharbal and Monomach also sat up. I noticed at once that Hannibal had not drunk.

'The elephant can't be far away,' he said, when I had made my report to him.

'An elephant lost?' Monomach shouted at me. 'Just let me get my hands on the driver! Are we to postpone the conquest of Rome because of him?' He began to roar with rage. Maharbal wanted to call up the mounted troops. 'With a few hundred horsemen we shall soon catch him.'

Hannibal's decision was different. 'The elephants shall arrange matters among themselves. The best thing to do would be to take Suru.'

'That was Carthalo's idea too,' I said.

'He understands elephants,' Hannibal declared, and this was high praise for Carthalo.

Monomach entered the debate again. 'And when do we march?'

'As soon as we've got the elephant back,' Hannibal assured him. 'I can't spare any of them.'

Then I ran back to Carthalo and Ittibal, and we three mounted Suru and rode away. It was beginning to get light. The track, which was marked out unmistakably by the chain, led us through one of the breaches in the palisade which the captain and his drunken company had made, and from there into open country.

'Arba wanted a bath,' Ittibal hazarded, when it became clear that the track was leading to the elephants' ford. But at the elephants' ford there was no Arba. Carthalo discovered that the track led along the river. The ground was somewhat difficult for riding, but from the back of the elephant it was easy to make out the track; the chain had torn off branches from the undergrowth. Suru was following the trail eagerly.

We rounded a bend. Suddenly Carthalo gave a low call to Suru to bring him to a halt. Suru was not to be restrained. Then Carthalo pointed ahead of us and we looked at one another in amazement; Arba was not alone—she had given birth to a calf elephant. The wind was against us, and although we weren't fifty yards away from her, she had not yet seen us. She had found a place in the river which was as shallow as it was at the ford. She was suckling the little one. In order to do this she had planted herself over a piece of rock, so that the baby elephant could put its forelegs on to the rock and reach her udder. Arba's hind-quarters were turned towards us. The sight made me laugh. Arba started and swung round. Her ears slapped back against the sides of her head. Her trunk struck the ground with a sharp noise. The baby elephant was frightened and slipped down from the rock. Arba was now so nervous that she scented danger where none was. She picked up the young animal with her trunk and moved hastily towards the river. She waded into the river until the water came up to the flanks of the young one. Then Suru gave an anxious cry. And now Arba collected herself and turned round. She put the little one down on the bank and stood behind it; it was clear that she didn't know what to do next. Suru walked up to the two as if he were the third member of the trio. Arba was still so nervous that she again moved off to take flight. But no sooner had she taken a few steps away from the little one than it let forth such a shrill trumpeting that even Suru started in alarm. Arba came back to the young one, and now she behaved as if neither Suru nor we three existed and as if

76

she and her baby were alone in the world. It was hungry and its hunger was stronger than its surprise that someone else had suddenly come upon the scene. It tried to find the udder, which in elephants is close behind the forelegs. But it tried in vain, because everything about it was still too small. Then the mother knelt down and it found what it was looking for. But when Arba stood up again it felt that it had not yet had enough and it began again to trumpet. Arba tried to withdraw from the little one, but it ran in front of her and barred her way. Arba tried to push it away. The little elephant, with its grey hide and thick tufts of hair on its head, didn't give in. It went on grumbling until its mother allowed it to suck its fill. Now Ittibal burst out laughing, but his laughter didn't disturb the little elephant.

'She's made a pretty fool of me,' Ittibal complained.

'Of us all,' Carthalo agreed. 'And we deserve it for not having kept our eyes open. But a thing like this isn't allowed for with war elephants.'

'And what now?' Ittibal looked helplessly at Carthalo.

'Back to the camp,' was Carthalo's suggestion. 'They must all see this. It's a sight worth seeing!' He let Suru go slowly up to Arba. The little elephant looked at him curiously. It sniffed at Suru's legs as if it were looking for an udder and then turned away disappointed. Suru put out his trunk to take hold of Arba's, and after some resistance Arba yielded hers to him. They both swung their heads as if they were taking counsel together. Then Suru started off. Arba followed him, and the little elephant ran along under its mother's body, in between the four tremendous pillars that carried Arba. But for most of the way Arba carried the little one in her trunk. It didn't cry again until we came in sight of the camp. There the mercenaries and drivers had been up and about for a long time. It was nearly midday. The little elephant stretched out its trunk doubtfully towards the strange smells which were carried on the wind from the camp, and when its cocked ears caught the unaccustomed noises it began to trumpet again. It refused to take a step farther.

Some men came out of the camp towards them, but Carthalo would not let them come right up to the elephants. Not until Hannibal appeared, attended by Maharbal, Monomach, and Silenos, did the look of anxiety leave Carthalo's face.

78

'No one understands elephants as well as he does,' said Carthalo.

'He'll swallow me whole!' Ittibal cried for the second time.

'You needn't be afraid,' said Carthalo consolingly. 'He wouldn't want to give himself indigestion.'

'This is a nice thing!' Monomach called from a distance.

Hannibal took a lump of salt out of his pocket, walked quietly up to Arba and held it out to her. Arba took it, put it into her mouth, and then began to wave her trunk. Now Hannibal held out his empty hand to the young elephant. The little animal, whose trunk hung down to one side as if it didn't properly belong to it yet, sniffed at the hand. It seemed to like the smell of it. It tried to get it into its little mouth. Hannibal enticed the little elephant two steps away from Arba. Its eyelids were still partly stuck together so that it could hardly see, and suddenly it stumbled and bounced up against Hannibal, who lost his balance and fell over on to the sandy ground. We burst into loud laughter. The noise frightened the little elephant, and it fled back to the shelter of its mother's body.

'He promises well,' Hannibal prophesied, picking himself up.

'Not a day old yet and he knocks Hannibal down!'

Hannibal was so taken with the little elephant that he didn't yet realize that a decision would have to be made.

Monomach reminded him of it: 'We shall never get him over the mountains.'

'I shouldn't dream of taking him,' said Hannibal. 'We should have him freezing to death.'

'He can't be left alone,' said Ittibal tentatively. He was watching Hannibal's face, as if he were waiting for judgement to be pronounced.

Hannibal was looking at Arba, the strongest she-elephant he had. 'We shall miss you,' he murmured at last.

Then Monomach flared up. 'Surely no one would sacrifice a well-trained elephant for the sake of a wretched little creature like that! Too much is at stake.'

'You are right,' said Hannibal, 'an elephant like this one is at stake.' Then he made a motion of his head towards Arba. 'You must see that the little one has mettle in him!'

'Supposing he has!' cried Monomach, letting his anger get the better of him. 'But he's no good to us now, and Arba is!'

Hannibal looked at him challengingly. 'Try if you like to separate them.' He stepped back, and now Monomach was standing close to Arba and her little one. It was as if the elephant had understood the challenge: her ears stood out from her head, and as soon as Monomach took a step towards the little one, she let out a growl. Then Hannibal, who knew what Monomach was capable of when he was angry, walked up to Arba and she grew calm again.

'But you were reckoning on forty,' said Monomach uncomfortably.

'Well then, let us conquer Rome with thirty-nine,' Hannibal said. He held his hand out to the little one again, but this time it didn't want to play. Then Hannibal turned back towards the camp and gave the order to march.

13

HANNIBAL's decision to leave Arba behind with her little one was welcomed whole-heartedly by the Indos, although each one of them would have said that his elephant was necessary for the coming campaign.

'He always does the right thing,' Carthalo summed up for them. The whole army thought so. No one worried over the fact that no fewer than thirty thousand men, mostly Ligurians, Balears and Numidians, were being left behind under the command of Hannibal's brother Hasdrubal to defend New Carthage, and that another army of the same size, consisting mostly of Spaniards, was being sent to Africa. No one had the slightest doubt about the success of the campaign. The mercenaries swore by their twenty-six-year-old general, and when he ordered them to march they obeyed without questioning.

Only the elephants held a palaver just before the march. As always before a change in their way of life, they assembled and put their heads together, and one after the other gave forth a rumbling sound from deep down in his chest. The drivers were used to this and were careful not to disturb these deliberations, which had something solemn about them.

'It's a custom that goes back to the time when they were free,' Carthalo explained to me. 'Let them do it. In the end they have to do what we ask of them. They've given up thinking any other thoughts but ours a long time ago. But they can't give up thinking altogether.'

Each day the army advanced a distance that could easily be covered in four or five hours. Hannibal was anxious to spare both men and beasts, so that their capacity should be kept at its highest pitch. He moved towards the Ebro, leaving the town of Onussa to one side. He generally rode one of his horses, all of them coal-black, fiery animals, who looked well with the scarlet cloak billowing over their hind-quarters. Now and again he allowed Suru to carry him, and on those occasions Carthalo gave up the driver's place to me: 'Because I know he likes it.'

With Hannibal all my shyness melted away. He loved jokes and when he talked of Carthage, which he had left as a nine-year-old boy and never seen again, he didn't tell me about Moloch or about the oath, but about the tricks he had played on his father's slaves. 'I often ran away down to the harbour and then they had to hunt for me on the ships.'

'I was happiest too when I could go down to the harbour and on to the ships,' I said.

'And now still?'

'Now I'm happiest when I'm on an elephant.'

And he said, 'It's the same with me.'

Sometimes Hannibal fell into a silence which the noise of the advancing army could not touch. Then neither Monomach nor Maharbal would ride up to him, nor even his brother Mago, who was only a few years older than I was and who was said to be Maharbal's right hand; nor would Silenos. I took good care not to interrupt the silence. Suru also joined in it; he was careful not to do anything that might make a shout necessary. Carthalo rode on Tembo who, now that Arba was no longer there, kept even closer to Suru than when they were in the winter camp.

One day Hannibal gave me a surprise. He began without any warning to talk. At first I thought he was telling me an old story, but I soon realized that it was a dream that haunted him.

'Someone who was like me in appearance made a sign to me to follow him without fear. I had no mercenaries behind me, not a single man, but instead of mercenaries I felt that there was something behind me far more powerful than an army. I didn't like to look behind me. I was afraid.'

'I can't believe that,' I exclaimed, looking him in the face.

'Listen!' He gave a quick smile and then went on: 'For a long time I didn't dare to look round. But then I began to feel as if a thunder-storm was bearing down on me from behind and that it might at any moment break out. Then I gave myself a push and looked round, and there was a thunder-cloud above me that took up half the sky; and as though it had been waiting for me to look at it, it burst asunder and brought forth a dragon which in its descent made the mountains tremble and rooted up trees and shrubs.'

In my mind's eye I saw the wood that Suru and the other elephants had laid low, and as I didn't know what a dragon looked like I pictured it to myself like a cloud of Berserks with horns and the heads of wild animals.

'It was like an avalanche of stones that buried everything in its course,' Hannibal went on, 'and the farther I rode behind the strange guide, who looked so like me, the more accustomed I grew to everything behind me being buried. The destruction in my rear spread such horror around me that no one dared get in my path.'

'It was the Berserks, it was the army!' I said, although I hadn't meant to say anything. I thought Hannibal would be angry with

82

me. But he only charged me to tell no one about the dream and to keep it to myself.

It was impossible to forget the dream. In those days I was proud that there was something that no one knew except him and me.

During the march the army seldom encamped. It was unlikely that the tribes through whose territory we passed would put up a resistance. Ravines and rivers were easily crossed. For the elephants the only obstacle was the Ebro. And even that they accepted in the end as an opportunity for a good bath. Suru, Tembo, and Rocco, the three leading elephants, approached the steep slope of the bank without any hesitation, stamped the edge down and so made a gentle slope over which all the elephants, one after another, slid down into the water. They tramped across the river with raised trunks. Only the Dwarf had to swim.

Among the mercenaries there were some who were more frightened of a rushing river than of the superior strength of an enemy. Hannibal swam twice across in order to pilot the timid ones to the opposite bank. He would not allow anyone to mock those who were afraid of the water. 'There is something special about water,' he said; 'it's worse for a man to be afraid of blood.' On such occasions it could be seen that he cared for each man as a person.

But there came a day when he sent three thousand men home. On the march through the territories of the Ilergetes, the Carpetani and the Bargusiri, many had declared themselves willing to take part in the march on Rome. But at the foot of the Pyrenees about five hundred Carpetani left the camp secretly, because on thinking it over, the way to Rome seemed after all rather long. The defection of these five hundred was reported to Hannibal. Everyone thought he would post sentinels round the two thousand five hundred Carpetani who were still in his army. He did the opposite. He dismissed them, and the whole army believed that Hannibal had sent all the Carpetani home because he didn't think well enough of them. The rest felt the sense of their own importance much heightened by this dismissal.

83

The Pyrenees were crossed near the coast. The elephants took the ravines and mountain ridges more easily than the foot and horse troops, and Hannibal made them take the lead up the steep slopes to tread steps for the others. On those occasions Suru was at the head of the procession, and Hannibal rode him as lightheartedly as if he were marching through protected country, instead of through regions which had never yet seen a Carthaginian army.

On the other side of the mountains Hannibal sent spies ahead.

While the army pitched camp near the town of Illiberis it was reported to Hannibal that the rumour was being spread over the countryside that the Carthaginians were advancing to subdue the land of Gaul. It was reported to him also that detachments of Celts had assembled in the neighbourhood at the town of Ruscino and that they were preparing to bar his way.

Monomach's opinion was that they should be swept into the sea. 'Two days—that's all it will cost us,' he estimated.

'And a few thousand men,' Hannibal added coldly. 'We should miss them when we got to Rome.'

Mago suggested that the Celts should be trampled to death by the elephants.

'I should be sorry to use them so,' answered Hannibal, leaving it in doubt whether he meant the elephants or the Gauls. He sent emissaries to Ruscino who understood the Gallic language and who were to tell the pugnacious chieftains that he was not coming as an enemy of the Gauls but rather as their friend. He was ready to come to their camp to speak with them, and to come without arms, accompanied only by an interpreter. He would be equally glad to receive them all as his guests, and he would not mind if they came armed and with an escort.

The chieftains came. Hannibal entertained them with the best food that his camp cooks could offer. He spared neither wine nor words, and both went to the heads of the chieftains. Each of them was given a horse and a spear set with precious stones. In the end it came to such a pitch that one of the chieftains went over into Hannibal's army, and the others without exception offered him mercenaries. The way to the Rhône was open, and half Gaul had been conquered in a few hours and without a battle.

During the next few days Hannibal was so little taken up with thoughts of war that he spent a few hours daily talking Greek with Silenos. He was mounted on Suru, and Silenos was riding at his side. Sometimes Hannibal dictated in Greek and Silenos wrote down what he said. Later I heard from Silenos that Hannibal was writing his history.

'And why in Greek and not in his own language?' I asked in surprise.

'Because he wants people all over the world to be able to read his book,' Silenos explained. 'How many people can understand Carthaginian?'

One day Hannibal suggested that Silenos should teach me Greek too. Carthalo was there when Hannibal made the proposal, and his face darkened. For a moment it looked as if he were going to object but he changed his mind; when Hannibal considered anything necessary Carthalo could not bring himself to question it. Besides this, his mistrust of Silenos, which had expressed itself so violently in the camp, had disappeared on the march. One day Carthalo surprised me by saying that he rated the Greeks very highly. It is true that he meant the Spartans, who served in the Carthaginian army and who were always put in the vanguard by Hannibal. But Carthalo came more and more to consider even Silenos as 'one of us'.

Moreover Silenos thought it better for me to learn Roman than Greek. He had already taught me some Roman words in the camp, and now he pretended that I knew the language and only needed to be reminded of the little that I had forgotten. Soon I was able to talk about simple things with him, and I even tried to make Suru understand me when I spoke Roman—and Suru understood.

14

IT was midsummer when the army reached the Rhône. Hannibal had announced his coming to the powerful tribe of the Volcae, whose territory was on both sides of the Rhône, and he had sent presents to their chieftains. But when we came to the great river we found that all their warriors had crossed over to the left bank and that they had taken many of their women and children and some of their belongings. The Volcae considered the Rhône a broad enough bar to Hannibal's advance. They had built fortifications on the other side, and were drawn up ready to repel with arms any aggressor who might dare to cross the river.

But the Volcae were not alone on the river bank. The Rhône was a busy highway for trade, and on it goods were carried inland from the great port at its mouth. Some of the little boats were made of wood, some of plaited grass, and many of the traders who had come as the servants of other men had settled

87

down on the banks and now plied their own trade. This turned out to be a piece of luck for Hannibal. The alarmed faces, which at first almost everyone in his army had directed towards the wide river, cleared up when about a hundred little boats presented themselves. The mercenaries were more frightened of the river than of the Volcae, but for Hannibal himself the Volcae were the more serious problem. He didn't allow himself to be rushed into crossing the river immediately, just to show that he felt equal to the Volcae. His aim was to battle a way over the Alps, not to waste his time with local tribes who would anyhow come under his dominion when he had conquered Rome. But as a battle was unavoidable in this case he would fight it with as few losses as possible.

So he gave the order to buy up all the available boats and to make rafts out of tree trunks at top speed in order to get as large a force as possible over the river at the first crossing, so that the Volcae would lose their appetite for battle. At the end of the third day the bank was completely filled up with rafts, light boats, and clumsily built canoes. The Volcae on the opposite bank were clearly expecting the crossing to be made at any moment. They kept their eyes fixed on our bank.

But in the meanwhile Hannibal had altered his plan of action. Some of the Volcae whom he had bribed with presents had come over to his side, and these led the Carthaginian horse troops a day's march up the river to a place where it was divided into two by an island. At that place they crossed over by night on roughly made rafts, and made their horses swim beside them on long reins. Their clothes and their weapons were stuffed into waterproof skin bags. Those who preferred to swim across the river held tight on to these bags, or to their round shields which danced on the waves like tiny boats. In a few hours, before the night was over, the whole company of horse had reached the other bank, unmolested and with hardly any losses. After a short rest they began to move towards the rear of the enemy, and as soon as they came within sight of them they sent up columns of smoke as a signal to Hannibal. Then he gave the order to the mercenaries to cross. For the first time the elephants were kept back. The larger and smaller boats made a line across the river to serve as a bar and to break the force of the current, and the rafts drifted only a little way out of their course. The Volcae ran backwards and forwards on the opposite bank uttering loud yells, they clashed their weapons and shields together over their heads and were prepared to throw themselves on the aggressors who were coming across the river towards them. But at that moment Hannibal's horsemen charged the Volcae in the rear; they ran about in helpless confusion, and as at the first moment many of them had been mown down, the others threw away their weapons and fled. Hannibal didn't let his men pursue them; he even forbade them to pick up the weapons which the Volcae had thrown down in their hurried flight. He wanted to prove to his defeated enemy that he didn't wish to destroy them, but rather to get them on to his side. Now the only thing that remained to be done was to get the thirty-nine elephants across. The tremendous noise which had come to them from the opposite bank had made them uneasy, and Hannibal didn't wish to hurry them. But a few of the drivers felt it a matter of pride to get their elephants across without delay, and one, in order to be the first, mounted his elephant and drove him into the river. The elephant waded on, even when the water rose as high as his back. The Indos took this quite calmly; he had often crossed rivers on the back of his animal. But suddenly the elephant dived; he blew out air, a column of water shot up, and the elephant disappeared. The Indos uttered pitiable cries; he couldn't swim and would have perished if he hadn't managed to clutch on to the elephant when he rose to the surface. The elephant climbed calmly out on to the bank and the Indos didn't make a second attempt to get his elephant across the Rhône. Another driver also wanted to distinguish himself. He teased his animal until the elephant began to run at him; the driver then ran ahead of him into the water, but the elephant turned back.

The elephants didn't want to swim across a river over which such terrible noises had come. Hannibal took counsel with the drivers. Finally he suggested that a road should be built farther down the river, where the elephants couldn't see it, and that it should lead into the river. But it wasn't to be an ordinary road, because the Rhône wouldn't put up with an ordinary road; it was to be a raft, seventy paces long and fifteen wide, covered with soil and turf, a disguised bridge, on which the elephants would have the feeling that they were on firm ground, even although there was river on both sides. A second raft, big enough to carry eight or ten elephants and ready to be pushed off, would be waiting for them at the end of the little tongue of land.

The Indos thought the plan was excellent. It took a day to make the tongue of land and the elephants' raft. The next morning the first eight elephants were led up to the disguised bridge. Hannibal was mounted on Suru so that he could overlook everything, but he chose not to lead the procession and let the she-elephants go on to the raft first; they were more docile, and Hannibal reckoned that the male elephants would be too proud to let themselves be outdone by the females.

One she-elephant after the other allowed herself to be driven on to the road, which had only been in existence a few hours. Clay had been trampled down on to the logs, bushes had been planted along the two edges. The elephants' raft was so large that it wasn't crowded, even when the last two elephants, one of whom was Suru, had stepped on to it. Now the boatmen stole on to the raft, carrying poles which had lain ready in the bushes. The ropes which had tied it to the bank were unfastened. The raft was caught in the current and floated off. The boatmen pushed it out into the river with their poles.

The elephants started violently, as though they had been struck by lightning. Their ears flapped back like the two wings of an opening gate, their trunks waved in the air. They looked about them for the enemy who had so treacherously removed the firm ground from under their feet. Their enormous bodies grew as rigid as rocks, rumbling noises were heard from within them, and finally Suru broke out into a shrill trumpeting. He was so excited that it was impossible to hold him, and he plunged into the river. Two other elephants followed him. Hannibal, the two other drivers, and I came up out of the water in the midst of the three elephants; we clung on to the raft. Now that they were in the water the elephants grew quieter; they stayed alongside the raft. Suru kept close to me. When he felt ground beneath his feet he came up a little farther out of the water and waded on with his trunk high in the air. When we had passed the middle of the stream I pulled myself up on to him by the saddle. Then several times in succession I said some words of praise into his ears, but he didn't reveal to me whether he was willing to be talked to. He came higher and higher out of the water and strode powerfully ahead of the other two elephants. When he got to the bank he made it plain that he was offended. As Hannibal went up to him Suru squirted a trunk-ful of water on to him to repay him for the shock he had given him.

'Am I not wet enough?' Hannibal asked him, shaking with laughter. Suru was appeased and that was the end of his sullen behaviour.

By the evening all the elephants had been brought over to the east bank. Carthalo, whom Hannibal had sent back with the empty raft, had been in favour of tying chickens or rabbits between the forelegs of the elephants to keep them quiet. But a few of the drivers hadn't let themselves be persuaded to do this, and several more elephants had jumped into the river. On the last journey the raft even overturned. This cost the lives of two boatmen, but the river had no other victims: all the elephants and their Indos were safe.

15

Now that the elephants had also been taken across the river, a few thousand Volcae, who had come back to find their lost weapons, joined the Carthaginian army.

Hannibal ordered a three days' rest. Entrenchments were

made, and the Volcae eagerly offered their help; they dug ditches and dragged up tree trunks. The elephants were given a holiday, and this time without any resistance they trotted down to the river as if they were paying a visit to an old friend. The mercenaries and the Volcae were beginning to barter their possessions with one another. A south wind was blowing that did everybody good. Weapons had been as carefully put aside as if they were not going to be used again in the foreseeable future. There was no more talk of war.

The elephants spent the whole day by the river. As in peacetime we played innocent tricks with them and they with one another. Carthalo romped with the Dwarf, frightened him by making deep buzzing noises, then let him chase him and made me jump on to the little elephant's back from behind. I slipped down on to his shoulders before he had begun to move and now I was where he couldn't shake me off. When he was preparing to lie down I jumped off and offered him some salt in the hope of reconciling him. The Dwarf refused it, although his Indos, the Giant, tried to persuade him to take it. I walked away with a bad conscience. Suddenly something struck me on the back. I turned round sharply; I thought the Dwarf had given me a whack with his trunk—but he was still standing where I had left him. The Giant burst out laughing and so did the other drivers who had been watching. Then I saw a lump of clay lying at my feet; it had bounced off me. The Dwarf had fired it after me and had hit me. Now everyone could see that he was satisfied. And I felt better.

At sunset we went back to the camp. We found it in great excitement. While digging a trench a group of Volcae had come upon an enormous skull. After we had tied up the elephants we went to the open space in front of Hannibal's tent where the skull was displayed. It was about half the height of a man. It stared at us out of one huge black hole. The men who had brought it assured us that it had been lighter to carry than we would have thought, but they confessed that at the first sight of it they too had had an uneasy feeling.

92

'A Cyclops' head.'

Someone had said that, and because no one knew what else to
say, the mercenaries who were standing round the uncanny
discovery could hardly doubt that it was the skull of a giant of
prehistoric times. Only Carthalo and one or two other Indos
shook their heads. They exchanged looks with one another and
finally Carthalo said, 'But how could an elephant have got to
the Rhône?'

'An elephant?' No one believed him.

Then Hannibal, accompanied by Silenos, came out of his tent.
He looked at the skull in astonishment.

'It was a man's depth underground,' announced the captain
who had superintended the trench-digging.

'Only an elephant has a skull as enormous as that, surely,'
maintained Hannibal.

'It *is* an elephant's skull,' Carthalo insisted. He went up to
the skull and began to demonstrate. 'What you think was the

Cyclops' eye was his trunk-hole.' He pointed to the tiny holes where the elephant's eyes had been.

Now everybody could picture the skull on an elephant.

'But how did an elephant get here?' asked Hannibal.

'It must have been dead a long time,' said Silenos.

In order to explain the skull Carthalo had taken hold of it, and it was in such a state of decay that a little piece of bone had crumbled off in his hand. The huge skull no longer looked awe-inspiring, and as no one could throw light on the problem of how an elephant's skull could have been found here by the Rhône, so far from the countries where elephants live, Carthalo's contention was now questioned again, and in the end everyone in the camp called the skull 'the Cyclops'.

Many looked upon it as an omen of disaster, and no one quite understood why Hannibal allowed it to be left lying outside his tent.

Towards evening a cloud of dust was seen in the south. It came rapidly nearer. Its appearance caused no one alarm, least of all Hannibal. That morning he had sent his young brother down-stream with three hundred horsemen to assure himself that no danger was advancing from that quarter. The port at the mouth of the river belonged to the Romans.

Now Mago came back. He and his followers rode into the camp on their exhausted horses, and the sweat of several of the horses was mixed with blood. Some of the riders were wounded too. And nearly every second rider was missing. Horses also were missing. In a flash the rumour spread over the camp: the Romans are coming! Mago rode straight to Hannibal's tent. I saw him coming, I was cleaning Hannibal's armour. Maharbal, Monomach and Silenos were with Hannibal.

Mago was pale when he entered the tent. There was blood on the left sleeve of his coat.

'You're wounded?' Hannibal sent for Synhal, and the doctor came at once.

'It's only a scratch, nothing more,' said Mago to quieten his brother's misgivings. But Hannibal insisted that Synhal should

94

attend to the wound. While the doctor washed and bandaged it Mago reported that towards noon he and his three hundred horsemen had come upon a company of about the same number of Romans. Neither party would give way to the other, and so both sides lost about half their men. 'When the wounded and riderless horses outnumbered the unhurt they caused a panic. They dragged the horses who still had riders along with them, and there was no holding them on either side. By Moloch! It was only thanks to the horses that anyone escaped, on their side as well as on ours.' Mago had kept his eyes on the ground during the making of his report; now he looked at Hannibal. 'We did our best to beat them.'

'It's something to be thankful for that I didn't give you the whole army,' said Hannibal with some sharpness in his tone.

'Ought we to have let them escape?' said Mago, on the defensive.

'You ought to have escaped yourself,' Hannibal corrected him, 'and to have brought back as many others as possible— particularly of the enemy.'

'We have brought two of them,' said Mago. 'Two wounded men fell into our hands.'

Hannibal's face cleared. 'I must question them at once.'

'They're more dead than alive,' Mago announced.

'Fetch them here!' Hannibal insisted. 'I must have them while there's any life left in them. It isn't much that I want to get out of them.'

The two prisoners were brought in on stretchers. They had lost blood and looked like dead men. Both were very young. Hannibal ordered them to be given wine. He talked to them in the Roman language.

'We are not Romans,' said one of them in Celtic. 'But our king is in league with the Romans, and he sold us to them.'

'Are many others of you in the Roman army?'

'Four hundred,' the same one said. 'This accursed war!' He groaned.

'It's over for you two,' Hannibal comforted him. 'As soon as

95

we've nursed you back to health I will give you horses.' He talked to the two prisoners as if they were his own men. Synhal was ordered to examine their wounds. In the meanwhile Hannibal questioned them and by the time they were carried out of the tent he knew that the Roman Consul Publius Cornelius Scipio had brought sixty war-ships into the harbour of Massilia, had landed there and was now setting up a camp of thirty thousand men to bar the Carthaginians' way to Rome.

'I don't suppose they could get more men on to their feet,' said Hannibal mockingly.

'So much the better,' was Monomach's opinion. 'None of those will escape us.'

'We ought to attack them before they have time to entrench themselves by the Rhône,' suggested Maharbal.

'For every one man that I lost at least three of them shall fall to the sword,' declared Mago with a distorted face.

'You're a damned lot of Roman-eaters!' said Hannibal in a tone that made the three others look up.

'You're not thinking of letting them off?' Monomach said excitedly.

'Them too,' said Hannibal, 'but above all ourselves.'

'Aren't we going to fight the Romans?'

'Not here,' said Hannibal, and his meaning was unmistakable. Then Monomach started up. 'Are we going to run away from them?'

'Yes,' said Hannibal, 'away over the mountains.'

Monomach was so dumbfounded that he sat down again.

Hannibal turned to Mago. 'How many of your three hundred did you lose?'

'Half,' said Mago sadly.

'To three hundred Romans!'

'They fought desperately for their lives,' Mago said in his own defence.

'That is a sure sign that the thirty thousand will throw down their arms as soon as ever they see us!' remarked Hannibal dryly. 'To win a victory over this Scipio would cost us a quarter of the army, if not more; and if the Romans dodge us, a fortnight into the bargain. By that time there would be no road over the Alps.'

Now the faces of Monomach, Maharbal, and Mago grew grave. Hannibal drove their gloom away with a few short sentences. 'We will fight and beat the Romans at Rome,' he declared. 'The Roman Consul who wants to bar our way will have his trouble for nothing. He can take possession of an empty camp. That's all he deserves. The victory he's offering us isn't a big enough one. We shall beat the Romans nearer home. To-morrow at dawn we move up the Rhône. Nothing shall prevent us from knocking before long at the gates of Rome.'

With these words all resistance melted away. When Maharbal, Monomach and Mago had gone, Hannibal took counsel with Silenos for a long time. 'There is no other way,' said Hannibal. 'We *must* go over the mountains. The sea belongs to Rome since they defeated us at sea. We old seafarers are now forced to fight them on land, outside their own gates.' He asked Silenos whether he knew anything about Scipio.

'As good as nothing,' Silenos confessed.

'There must be something about the man,' said Hannibal, 'or they wouldn't send him against me.'

16

AT dawn the next morning the march began again. The elephants were in front. Hannibal was riding one of his horses; and with a little company of horsemen was reconnoitring and leading the way. We met scarcely any obstacles and made good progress, likewise on the second and third day of our march up the river.

The army was low-spirited. In spite of the heavy losses that Mago had suffered on his reconnoitring expedition the mercenaries were in favour of getting to grips with the Romans at once. No one approved of Hannibal's decision to evade them.

On the evening of the third day the ambassadors of a certain Branco presented themselves before Hannibal. Branco called himself King of the island Inis and offered his friendship. Less than two hours later more ambassadors arrived, 'from the King of Inis', but this time his name was Colchas. As soon as Branco's men saw the men of Colchas they began to let fly at one another. It turned out that Branco and Colchas were brothers.

'Branco has always been king,' said the first comers.

'Colchas is a better king,' said the others.

They were just going to charge one another with their spears. Hannibal heard what both sides had to say and decided for Branco. He gave Branco's ambassadors presents to take back with them. He told the men of Colchas in no uncertain terms that unless Colchas would quit the field of his own accord, he himself would treat him as a rebel and dispatch him to a country from which there would be no return. 'This is just how it should be,' said Hannibal to his councillors; 'everyone quarrelling for our friendship.'

'Why did you decide for Branco?' asked Mago.

'Because of those trees over there,' explained Hannibal. He pointed to a group of trees about a hundred paces away. 'I was so tired of listening to what the ambassadors had to say that I began to count the trees: Colchas—Branco—Colchas—Branco . . . It came to Branco. That will cost the island king something.'

After another day's march we reached Inis. It was not a real island, as we discovered in the next few days, but a large piece of land, bounded by the Rhône on one side and by a rushing river called the Arar on the other. The northern boundary was a range of hills which stretched from the Rhône to the Arar.

'Could be defended by a handful of good men,' estimated Hannibal, 'and impossible to starve out.'

It was alluvial land, periodically flooded. Everything that man needed grew there in profusion. Hannibal decided to stay there a few days, to rest the army and to replenish his stores.

In the four months since the army had been on the march it had covered nearly six thousand furlongs. It had grown larger on the way. But the severe test was still to come; everyone in the army felt that. Autumn was coming. During the last few days the air had been very clear. On the eastern horizon there was a white bar: the mountains with snow on them all the year round. The mercenaries often looked towards them, and although they had everything they wanted on the island, there was not the same gaiety now that there had been in the camp outside New Carthage. At night-time a wind blew from the mountains, and it tasted of snow.

Hannibal saw that many of his men were tormented by doubts. Maharbal, Monomach, and Mago urged him to talk to the mercenaries, but he wouldn't listen to them.

On the fourth day, the last the army was to spend on the island, a company of horsemen rode up from the east and presented themselves in the camp. The news spread like wildfire through the camp: 'Horsemen from beyond the Alps are with Hannibal!' Soon the army had formed a circle round the leader of these horsemen. He was a fair-haired giant who towered over Hannibal.

Hannibal spoke first. He said: 'This is Magal, one of the kings of the Boii. He has come over the mountains to meet us. In the land where his people live they have heard the news that we are coming. Magal brings us good news. Not only his people but other tribes as well are prepared to march with us against the Romans. The revolt has already begun. When Roman land surveyors appeared in the country of the Insubres, in order to choose sites for new Roman towns, they were slaughtered and the garrisons of the neighbouring Roman fortresses were driven away. It is time for us to come, says King Magal; they are waiting for us. Let him speak for himself!'

Magal stepped forward and threw his head back, so that he looked still taller. He spoke loudly and as he spoke he opened his mouth wide. Only a few understood him, and he came within a hair's breadth of being laughed at. Hannibal intervened in the nick of time and translated what he had said: 'Now perhaps you are worrying about the road that lies before you. That whiteness under the sky that's looking across to you frightens you. Let me tell you: we too travelled over the mountains, not with elephants like you but with our wives and children. Belloves led his people over the Taurian pass; Elitori led the Cenomani over the Alps; the Boii, the Ligures, the Senones all climbed over the mountains, and only twenty years ago Atis and Galatas, kings of the Boii, brought their peoples to the south. Concolitan climbed up from the Rhône with his people, as you are about to do. There is no lack of roads and guides. Men and women live up there in the mountain valleys as they do everywhere else. There are no mountains that reach up to the sky.'

Hannibal pointed to Magal and to his companions. 'They have ridden the way that we shall ride!' he cried. 'Or do you believe that they came over the mountains on wings?'

Magal opened his mouth again and shouted a few sentences very loudly. He had stretched out his arm towards the elephants. Hannibal repeated Magal's words: 'Have you not mountains of your own with you: your elephants? When you come down from the mountains with them the Romans will run so fast that you won't be able to catch them.'

Then once again it was as it had been four months ago at the beginning of the march; the army shouted as one man: 'Hannibal is right!'

'We will receive you like brothers,' Magal assured them, overwhelmed by so much ardour. 'Wherever I go they shall hear the truth from me about Hannibal's army,' he promised. It was with difficulty that Hannibal persuaded him to be his guest for one day.

The last day on the island was a day of festivity. The mercenaries were intoxicated by the thought that they were expected beyond the mountains. Now jokes were made about the mountains. 'When our elephants charge them they will give way!'

The elephants were the only ones whose heads were cool.

100

And when the march began at dawn they moved silently out of the camp. A line of grey hills was advancing with a gentle roll towards the mountains.

17

FOR ten days now we had a river on our left: first the Rhône, then the Arar, and on our right walls of rock, which were often so close to the river that it seemed impossible for us to get through. But there was a way, and the army accustomed itself to marching between rock and river. Branco had given us horsemen who rode at the head of the procession, and they played the part of mediators when it was necessary to reassure the tribes through whose territories we passed. So we arrived without losses at the Druenta, a mountain torrent which falls into the Arar. This torrent was now to be crossed.

The river was not wide: our slingers could hit the trees on the other side when they tried—but mercenaries and horse, and also the elephants, were afraid of approaching its bank. Branco's men didn't hide from us that it was a treacherous river sprinkled with banks of shingle, and full of whirlpools—not a river for boats, nor even for rafts!

Nevertheless Hannibal tried it with rafts. But the first raft was sucked into a whirlpool, it overturned and eleven mercenaries were drowned. Then Hannibal ordered several of the fords to be planted with stakes at regular distances and the stakes to be joined to one another by leather straps, so that there might be fences for the men to hold on to when they crossed the river. But while building these fences several more men were swept away by the river and lost their lives. The water tasted of ice.

The mercenaries looked over the fences at the mountains, which had grown higher and higher as the army had drawn nearer to them. Now it looked as if they took up half the sky. Right at the top of them was ice and the sky seemed to be sticking to it. The shreds of cloud which hung down over the mountain-tops were the colour of dirty snow. The air was cold and cut like a knife. The men cursed and wished themselves back by the Rhône, in a straightforward battle, with Romans to reckon with and not the invisible devils who had piled up this black hell.

Clothes and weapons were once again stuffed into bags of hide, and now the river had to be crossed. Hannibal was one of the first. Fires were lighted on the other side and the men could dry themselves. The fences played the part that Hannibal had promised himself they would play.

For the elephants the fences were out of the question. Besides, it was impossible anyhow to lead them across to the burning mounds on the opposite bank which had already made them uneasy. A place in the river was discovered by some of the drivers which might serve as an elephants' crossing. As at the Rhône a beginning was made with a few she-elephants, but this time without rafts.

At first the elephants would not go into the water; two turned round, but finally three took the risk and waded into the river. At every step they felt cautiously for a safe foothold. All went well and they arrived safe and sound on the other bank. But nothing could persuade the two who had turned round to enter the water. Only the Dwarf went across, after the Giant had found him a way, but in places he had to swim.

Then Carthalo proposed that the remaining thirty-five elephants should be driven all together into the river, so close to one another that breaking loose would be out of the question. Everyone agreed, and the elephants were drawn up in three rows, with Suru and Rocco on the outsides of the first row.

The elephants moved forward step by step. The swollen river, which came up to their flanks, and still more the fear of the icy water, kept them pressed close to one another. Like an unbroken island, composed of grey hills, they came to the middle of the river, and then on a bit farther. But suddenly four or five elephants lost their foothold on a shingle bank; they fell and

pulled some of the others down with them, and the result was a panic that it was impossible to control. Every driver thought only of his own elephant and himself. Carthalo who was sitting behind me roared at Suru, but as all the Indos were shouting, and as some of the elephants were beginning to trumpet in their alarm, every word was drowned. Suru stood in the water like a rock. He only began to move again when he felt that there was no other elephant at his side. He put down one foot after the other hesitatingly. He had thrown his trunk back; the tip of it lay between the two enormous humps on his forehead. Now that Suru had begun to move Carthalo stopped shouting. Suru took so long to take one step that Carthalo beat me on the shoulders in his impatience. At last Suru was only three or four steps away from the other bank. But now he stopped again. Carthalo spoke to him; he beat him on the ears with his stick. And then he did what he had never done since I had ridden Suru: he seized the iron hook that hung from the saddle and thrust the point of it into the elephant just behind his ear. The shock forced Suru to take another step. Then he stumbled and flung Carthalo and me into the river. I got hold of his tusk which was sticking out of the water and clung on to it. I felt gravel under my feet and could walk on it, but Suru was trying desperately to get a firm hold with his forefeet. He was getting beside himself with fear; he even tried to shake me off and got more and more embroiled with the shingle bank. I was swept away. Carthalo pulled me out on to the bank.

'He would have trampled you to death,' he panted; 'when he's like this, it's as if you and I didn't exist.'

Carthalo ran for boughs of trees and threw them to Suru, but they were washed away by the river before Suru could pick them up with his trunk. I wanted to go back into the water to Suru, but Carthalo held me back firmly. 'It's no good!' he panted. 'No one but himself can help him.'

I felt as if I were standing in ice. I looked at Suru. He was not giving up the fight for his life. Struggling bravely on, he pushed himself forward until he had left the whole shingle bank behind

104

him and had found firm ground for one forefoot. He then drew the other foot up, and putting his weight on it pulled himself out. The front part of his body towered like a giant out of the water. And now he began to trumpet, but this time there was no fear in his trumpeting.

Never before had Suru seemed to me so heroic as now when he came out on to the bank. There he stood risen from the dead. Carthalo was still holding me back. 'Don't go to him!' he warned. But I broke away, and in a few strides I was close to Suru, threw my arms round the leg with which he had first stepped on to firm ground, and wept and was not ashamed of my tears.

Five Indos and four elephants lost their lives in that river. When Hannibal heard the news he turned pale, and after Carthalo had told him the whole story he turned away and stared at the steep mountain-side in front of him. When after a little while he turned his face towards us again he noticed that we were shivering. 'Sit down by the fire, you'll catch your death of cold,' he said. His voice was hoarse.

The elephants had been left untethered in order that they might move about and dry more quickly. The drivers were sitting round the fires, turning first their faces, then their backs to the flames. They were gradually recovering their equilibrium.

It took the elephants longer; it was several hours before they had recovered from the shock. Only a few of them collected into groups in order that they might warm one another. In some cases it was clear that they were looking for a friend who had been washed away by the river.

Towards evening something unexpected happened: Suru and Rocco met one another. Suddenly they both began to growl. Then as though they had been impelled by invisible drivers they went for one another. Now they stood head to head and each tried to push the other away. The horrified drivers jumped up. At first Carthalo and Gisgo wanted to go to the enraged elephants, but soon they both came to the conclusion that it was better to let the two male elephants fight it out. Everyone

H

realized that it was a battle to decide who should be head of the herd during the march over the mountains.

Suru and Rocco were about equally strong. Suru had only one tusk, but on the other hand his trunk was considerably stronger, and with his trunk he tried to get hold of Rocco's head. Rocco escaped him and then made a fresh charge. The two giants pressed heavily upon one another; their bodies quivered all over. One forehead grated against the other; it sounded as if something between them was being ground to pieces.

'Stop them!' demanded some of the Indos, who were getting more and more uneasy as they watched. Carthalo refused to interfere and Gisgo explained that it would only become dangerous if one of the two turned tail. So long as neither of the two elephants turned to take flight the other couldn't do damage to him with his tusks—that we all knew.

'It must be decided sooner or later,' said Rocco's driver excitedly. He was sure of victory. Rocco had managed to push Suru back a few inches and it looked as if Suru would have to quit the field. Then Suru unexpectedly gave way a little to one side, and Rocco stumbled, slipping along Suru's flank. His knees gave. Suru also stumbled. Both got on to their feet again at the same moment and took up their positions again for battle. Now each elephant was standing on the side that had at first belonged to the other. And now they charged one another, not with lowered heads but with their trunks raised. Both dealt powerful blows. Trunks landed with loud slaps on heads and trunks. And then, just as Rocco was raising his trunk to strike again, Suru's trunk whizzed through the air and fell on to Rocco's tusks with such enormous force that both broke off. Rocco was stunned. It was a terrifying sight for all the onlookers. The broken tusks were bleeding at the stumps.

In his bewilderment Rocco lifted his trunk to his mouth and put the tip of it inside. He turned away and walked to the river. There he washed his chest and flanks as thoroughly as if they had been covered with dirt. Suru left him alone. He turned his back

108

on him, raised his trunk high up in the air, and proclaimed his victory loudly. The other elephants assembled round him.

Rocco was washing himself; he was washing his shame off. His Indos, and Carthalo too, went to him, and both offered him salt when he came out of the water. Rocco took it from both. His pride was broken.

'It needn't have ended like that,' said Carthalo, and his voice sounded as if he were asking pardon. 'But it had to be decided sooner or later.'

Gisgo was of the same opinion. As for the bleeding nerve ends, Carthalo comforted Gisgo. 'I've had that before. In time they'll draw back into the head. He won't die of that.'

At that moment Rocco sneezed. Carthalo and Gisgo jumped away in alarm. All the elephants started. Rocco didn't dare to join the herd. Even when night fell he stayed alone. His Indos lay down at his feet to sleep, rolled in a blanket. At early dawn he woke up cold. Rocco had gone. His track led into the river. When we woke up we saw Rocco's driver crouching like a lump of rock on the bank. Hannibal gave him the elephant whose Indos had been drowned.

18

WE now set out again with thirty-four elephants. Suru led the procession. One elephant followed the other, and each laid his trunk on the back of the one in front of him. The line of elephants moved silently up towards the mountains.

Hannibal had sent a strong troop of horse ahead as vanguard. We could see the men dismount as it grew steeper. They led their horses by the bridle. They still had with them four of the men who had served as guides since we left the 'island', and they assured everyone that no attack was to be feared as long as there was space enough between the mountains to elude the enemy.

The mountains drew nearer, from in front, from the left, and from the right. They grew tall before our eyes. They were not like mountains as we knew them. Huts were perched on the steep slopes, like frozen birds with stiffly spread wings. Cows, pressed close to one another to avoid the cold, were sheltering under overhanging rocks. Everything looked strange and threatening, and the summits with their white edges cut off more and more of the sky. We heard strange cries from high up. Nothing moved and this was just what made us uneasy: round about us everything was dead and yet everything was on the watch.

And then suddenly the tops of the mountains disappeared. They were drowned in a bank of clouds. A heavy veil was drawn over the rest of the sky. It began to rain. The rain washed the road away; our vanguard disappeared in the clouds. The mountains had put on their invisible cap. They had gone, and yet we knew that they were there.

Hannibal rode past us. He was urging his horse on in order to catch up the vanguard. In an hour's time we also came up to them. Hannibal called his captains together. He climbed on to Suru so that all of us could see him while he talked to us.

'We must be prepared to come upon the enemy,' he announced. 'The rain has swallowed up our friends who have so far shown us the way. It was getting too dangerous for them. Now I have heard from Magal that the mountain folk, with whom we have to reckon, are tremendous sleepers and that they do not fight at night-time or in a mist, but only by daylight. In any case then the nights belong to us, and with regard to the mist—we shall see. We must try to get up out of this valley, so that we can spit on to their heads, not they on to ours.'

The march began again. The elephants were now put in the middle. Maharbal and Mago were at the head. Hannibal kept near the elephants, and Monomach marched with his most tried and trusty mercenaries in the rear so that the procession could not be folded up from behind. Visibility was still bad.

Carthalo cursed. He said scornfully, 'They don't bear thinking of! There's nothing more pitiable than the man who runs away! A coward doesn't deserve to live.'

I was infected by Carthalo's anger.

'Leaving Hannibal in the lurch like this—Hannibal!' Carthalo complained. 'None of his men would do that. You will see how they fight for him.'

I remembered the cloud of Berserkers. How they had rushed at one another on that sandy plain! It wasn't difficult for me to imagine Monomach charging the ranks of the enemy.

The rain made our track slippery. Suru put each foot down carefully. He walked with the utmost attention, as if he had put out feelers far ahead into the wet veils of mist. The road led along the right-hand slope of the mountain; it was not immoderately steep. On our left the ground dropped away—how far it was impossible to tell in the heavy rain. We looked up the slope, but above us it was lost in cloud. The clouds, the precipice, the opposite mountain-slope—everything was uncannily still. The mountains were silent. Everyone knew that there was now no possibility of avoiding the enemy. Then one of the elephants dislodged a stone. It leapt away and with it an avalanche of stones went thundering down into the valley. Then the deathly silence began again. Suru was now taking bigger steps. He was afraid, and I felt that his fear was growing. I myself was afraid and looked at Carthalo.

'There's no need to be frightened,' said Carthalo, and his voice was hoarse.

Then we heard the dull beats of a stone coming down to us from above. It must have been an enormous fragment. Men and animals started in alarm. The procession came to a standstill. Suru was standing as though he had once and for all reached the spot to which his last step had brought him. His ears were standing back like boards and his trunk was pointing up the mountain-slope.

The fragment of rock rolled down between the fourth and fifth elephants; it did no one any harm. But some of the elephants lost their heads; they tried to turn round, which was difficult on

III

the narrow track, or they tried to escape down the slope. One of them slipped, turned a somersault, and fell in the track of the rock.

The Indos did their utmost to quieten the elephants. The animals only grew more excited. Then Suru began to trumpet, and his summons was more powerful than the orders of any Indos. The elephants tried to gather together.

But now large and small stones began to roll down the mountain-side. Men and animals were hit. Cries filled the air. The mercenaries were given the order to climb up the slope. The wet shallow grassy soil gave them a poor hold. Wounded by the stones, mercenaries and horses hurtled down the steep slope. The worst confusion was in the baggage-train. Pack-horses went off the track in their alarm, lost their balance, and fell with their loads.

'This is hell!' cried Carthalo.

The procession, wedged in between mountain-slope and precipice, could neither retire nor defend itself. There was nothing to be seen of the enemy who was doing us all this damage. We were at his mercy, and the only thing left to us to do was to be frightened. For a moment I had the crazy idea that it was the mountains themselves that were trying to shake us off.

In my fear I had slipped off Suru's back and had taken refuge between his two forelegs. I was trembling. Was this what war looked like? It was quite different from what we had known on the sandy plain. I looked up at Suru. He had his trunk in his mouth—he too was frightened. As long as the terrible stones came down the slope I never stopped thinking: If only it doesn't hit Suru, only not Suru! I don't know how long I was hiding under Suru. Then I saw him take his trunk out of his mouth and hold it out to a man who was coming towards him. A hand was put out to me and pulled me out from between the elephant's legs.

'What are you doing down there?' It was Hannibal.

I looked up at him wildly. 'Is it over?'

'It's only just beginning,' he answered. His eyes were sparkling. I was listening. What more was coming down from up there?

'There won't be any more,' Hannibal assured me. 'They've thrown down everything they've got. Now they're going to sleep—until we wake them!'

The mercenaries were crowding round Hannibal. One of them was bleeding from the forehead.

'What a pack of cowards!' said Hannibal, pointing up the slope. 'They let the mountains down on us and then they creep away into their hiding-places.' He put his hand on the wounded man's shoulder. 'They shall pay dearly for your wound. Tomorrow we shall be spitting on to *their* heads.'

Now the Indos who had lost their elephants made their way to the front. There were six of them. Two more drivers had fallen with their elephants into the abyss.

'Tomorrow we'll throw them down,' said Hannibal, clenching his teeth. He climbed on to Suru and insisted that I should sit on the driver's saddle. 'You walk in front,' he said to Carthalo, 'we won't give Suru too much to carry. I've got a lot more for him to do.'

We rode off. 'And for you,' he said to me.

'I was afraid,' I said ruefully.

'So was I,' said Hannibal. 'But one can't be frightened for ever.' He struck me lightly on the shoulder. 'Are you still afraid?'

'No,' I said. It was not a lie. My fear had gone since Hannibal had been sitting behind me.

19

IT stopped raining. In half an hour's time we came out on to a plateau where there was enough room for a camp. It grew dark quickly. There was still nothing to be seen of the enemy. Hannibal ordered camp-fires to be lighted and to be left burning all night. Not one of them was to be allowed to go out, so that from up above us it would look as if no one had left the camp. At nightfall Hannibal set out with a band of picked mercenaries—six hundred in all—in the utmost secrecy and climbed the heights from which the mountain folk had rolled the stones.

'He'll pay them back!' Carthalo whispered to me, as he lay down beside me to sleep. The Indos lay in a wide circle round the elephants who had collected round Suru. There were still twenty-six elephants—eight had fallen into the abyss. It was impossible to reckon how many men and horses lay at the bottom.

Once during the night I started up. I had heard the cries of men and horses. I felt a cold hand thrust into my face. But it was nothing, it was only a dream. It had grown colder and before I went to sleep again I saw the stars shining. In the morning it was clear. The mountains round us were sparkling.

We could see the mountain folk making ready to take up the position which they had held the day before. They were coming out of their huts and climbing up to the heights.

Suddenly these heights came to life. Hannibal with his six hundred men charged down upon the stupefied mountain folk. There was a hail of spears. The surprised enemy was driven down the mountain. The mercenaries had blocked the way. Every rock was a death-trap, every ditch an ambush.

Towards midday, when the procession began to move again, there was no more need to fear that stones would roll down upon us. The heights belonged to Hannibal, so did the ravine and the slope. Smoking huts proclaimed that he had taken possession of them also. After a two hours' climb the procession came in sight of a fortified place which served the mountain folk as a refuge in time of war. Horsemen were sent ahead. They rode unopposed into the enclosure. It was in a sheltered valley and the land was cultivated. There were cattle in the meadows, and when the houses were searched so many supplies were found that the army would have enough to live on for at least three days. There was only one thing missing—inhabitants. Either they were

slain or they had flown; they had left all their possessions un-
guarded. Hannibal ordered the provisions to be distributed
among the mercenaries. The cattle were brought in from pasture
and slaughtered, as far as they weren't needed for the baggage-
train. There was plenty of fodder for our own animals. Nevertheless no one felt quite at ease in the deserted huts.

The elephants fended for themselves. I came upon Suru with
a leather bag full of salt which he couldn't lash open and which
he was throwing up into the air until it burst. The other elephants came up and took their share. Tembo was caught taking
the roof off a hut in order to get at the dried fruits stored among
the rafters. When his Indos gave him a blow with a stick on his
hind-quarters, Tembo made a face like a boy who had been
caught stealing, and put the tip of his trunk in his mouth in his
confusion.

The mercenaries made a systematic search and came upon
wine. As they were in any case intoxicated by the victory over
the mountain folk, it didn't take much wine to make the terrors
that they had survived look small and the summits ahead of them

ridiculous. Hadn't Hannibal pounced like a bird of prey on his enemy? There was no enemy left now! They seemed to have forgotten what the victory had cost. The survivors had been counted. The two thousand men, the four hundred horses, and the eight elephants that the abyss had swallowed up—and the three hundred men who in the battle that morning had fallen at the hands of the grim mountain warriors—seemed not to weigh in the balance, nor even the large number of wounded for whom it would be impossible to climb farther. They were tended as far as it was possible, and Hannibal bequeathed the stronghold to them.

There were dogs in this settlement who had not run away. The mercenaries threw them their refuse and the dogs soon lost all their timidity. They even dared to go close up to the elephants. And now we noticed that the grey giants went out of the way of the strange dogs—exactly as if they had been cats. And when a dog barked at an elephant, the elephant arched his back —exactly like a cat. But if a dog overstepped the mark, it might happen that he was hit by a trunk.

One day a man was struck down by an elephant. Before the driver had been able to stop it, it had happened. The man, a Berserker, had walked up to the elephant and had offered him a handful of dried fruits; the elephant had lifted his trunk as if he was going to take it and had dealt the man such a blow that he had collapsed on to the ground. When the elephant did that he usually went on to stab his victim with his tusks or to crush him with his knees. This elephant didn't do that. He turned his back on the man he had thrown to the ground and trotted away as though nothing had happened.

Indos and mercenaries ran up. 'He is dead,' said one. But the Berserker recovered his senses, and after a while was so much better that he could be helped on to his feet again.

The Indos asked for pardon: 'My elephant has never done that before.'

'It's my fault,' said the Berserker to everyone's astonishment. 'The day before the march out of the winter camp I tried to pick him up from the ground, and now I wanted to find out whether he had forgotten, but he has a damned good memory.'

The driver asked him to drink with him, 'To the elephant who spared your life!'

'Anything you like,' said the Berserker, who couldn't believe that he was still alive.

Something else happened on that day that was talked of for a long time afterwards. An elephant that had been given up for dead suddenly appeared in the settlement. He wandered all over the camp until he found his Indos. When the driver saw his elephant he stood rooted to the ground. The elephant put his trunk round the man's shoulder and shook him in order to make him believe that it was not a ghost he was seeing before him.

Hannibal came at once and greeted the home-comer round whom all the drivers and many of the mercenaries had collected. The elephant was wounded but no one noticed this who didn't look closely. At the place where his skin had been rubbed off by the fall the elephant had put a patch of clay.

118

'He knows how to look after himself,' said Hannibal admiringly. 'You can't kill him. Let him be an example to you!'

Hannibal asked for choice foods to be brought and fed him with them. 'He shall have a double salt ration,' he ordered. 'You don't know how valuable you are,' he said to the elephant. 'Or do you? Did you get yourself up out of the ravine because you did know?' He turned to the mercenaries and to the Indos. 'And if we arrived with only five elephants we should have half Italy in our pocket.'

Hannibal could see by their faces that no one had understood him.

'The Romans know that we're coming with elephants,' he explained. 'They're so afraid of elephants that they creep away into hiding-places in the mountains, because they think that they would be more easily caught by elephants on the plains. Well then, the plains belong to us even before we get there.'

The Indos and the mercenaries heard this with satisfaction. But one asked, 'And why, if the Romans think so much of elephants, don't they have them in their own legions?'

'That's easy to answer,' said Hannibal; 'because elephants can't bear the smell of Romans.'

Then Hannibal was sent for. In one of the houses someone had been found. Hannibal went at once to the house and I ran with him.

It was a poor-looking house, built of wood like all the others. The mercenaries had so far overlooked it or they had thought there was nothing in it worthy of attention. Now a few of them had entered the house and had found someone sitting by the hearth.

'He's so old that we can't tell whether it's a man or a woman,' one of the mercenaries reported, 'and perhaps he's dead; he doesn't move.'

Hannibal went into the house. I kept close to him and could see everything. The room was empty except for the hearth and a bench beside it. On the bench someone was sitting with white hair hanging down over his face.

'Who are you?' asked Hannibal, using Celtic words.

Then the face raised itself. A hand which was only skin and bone pushed the hair back from the temples. It was a woman. And then something happened that no one had expected. The aged woman stood up. She swept her hand over the hearth and cleared the ashes away. A red glow appeared, and the old woman took two handfuls of the glowing substance and held them out to Hannibal, who drew back in alarm.

'There, eat it!' said the old woman. The red substance fell to the ground which was made of trampled clay. The old woman stared at us in such a way that I began to wonder whether she had eyes at all.

'Let her alone, she is crazy,' said Hannibal and turned away to go. 'She won't do anyone any harm.'

That night the house in which the aged woman lived went up in flames. The fire spread so quickly that soon almost the whole settlement was burnt down. There were no homes left for the wounded.

The fire had not been able to get at the army. Tents had been set up round the outside of the settlement for the mercenaries, and most of the captured provisions had been taken out of the settlement, which from the beginning had had something uncanny about it for everyone.

The elephants had settled down for the night in a hollow where they would be protected from the wind. They didn't see the fire. The reflection of it which played over the sky and the mountain-side in a ghostly fashion, and the crackling of the flames, made the elephants uneasy, but the drivers were able to prevent a stampede. Suru and one or two others behaved as if there was nothing to fear. They were not mistaken—the fire held no dangers for the elephants.

When at last the settlement had been reduced to a black waste the twenty-seven grey giants were standing ready for the march. This time Hannibal put them in front. At dawn the procession began to move. It was the fourth day since the ascent had begun. It was a clear day. The mountains seemed deserted.

20

BUT there were still human beings; even some men were left. Towards midday in the full noon sunshine a company of people came to meet the procession. There wasn't much of them to be seen. They were carrying branches in front of them.

'Don't they want us to see who they are?' asked Hannibal who was sitting behind me on Suru.

At last eight elderly men came out from behind the walking bushes.

'Beggars!' was Hannibal's verdict when he saw them. 'They've come to ask for peace.'

He didn't dismount from Suru when the eight old men had come up to him. Maharbal, Monomach, Silenos and Mago, all on horseback, rode up to the front. The eight, surrounded by horsemen, looked anxiously up at Hannibal, and the eldest of them said, 'We belong to the same people as the men who have taken up arms against you. We too are Allobroges, but we are no longer against you. That black waste land which lies now where yesterday there was a large settlement has taught us a lesson. Your gods must be more powerful than ours. Therefore we will not tempt your superior strength but rather serve you. You want to cross the mountains where we are at home. We know the passes and we know which roads are the best for an army. If you wish, we will lead you to the pass which gives men and animals the least trouble. And if by chance there are still mountain folk who are against you we will make them change their minds.' The eight men laid the branches at Suru's feet and the eldest one said, 'These branches are signs of our friendship. We beg you to accept them.'

Hannibal was in no hurry to answer. But Suru seized the branches without any hesitation and devoured them with great satisfaction. The face of the eldest one cleared; he said eagerly, 'He accepts what we have brought for him; he is our friend.'

'Don't delude yourselves,' said Hannibal in the Carthaginian language; 'he's accepting the branches, not you.' Then he said in Celtic, 'If everyone else would meet us half-way as you have done, there would be no dead men in the ravines. If you want to make amends for the wrong done—we have nothing against it. Lead us to the pass!'

The old men were evidently glad that their offer had been accepted. In a moment the news spread all along the procession that experienced guides had presented themselves to Hannibal, and the mood of the army became definitely more cheerful. No one took the men seriously as negotiators. For whom could they have spoken? For wives and children who had fled? All the men capable of bearing arms had been put out of the way. But these men were invaluable as guides in the mountain wilderness, so thought everybody.

The men walked at the head of the procession. Hannibal dropped gradually behind, and when there was enough distance between him and the men he took counsel with his special advisers as he rode.

'What do you think of them?'

'Their fear of us stands us in good stead,' remarked Monomach. 'With regard to the road nothing serious can happen to us now.'

Maharbal and Mago thought the same.

'And you?' Hannibal asked Silenos.

'Their faces were hidden,' said Silenos.

'Only while they were coming towards us,' Mago remarked, 'but after they had put aside the branches——'

'Then more than ever,' Hannibal interrupted him. 'These old men remind me of certain Carthaginians, of Hanno's men.'

'But nevertheless you are trusting them?'

'I am letting them go ahead of us because they know the roads,' said Hannibal. 'But I am keeping an eye on them. And I am hoping to be able to read from their backs if they begin to lead us astray; it's impossible to read anything from their faces.'

122

'If they're foxes we'll skin them,' declared Monomach with a malicious smile.

'I would gladly do without their skins,' said Hannibal. He gave orders that the heights that they were about to climb should be kept under close inspection. Then he and Suru moved closer up to the old men, who seemed to find the climb no difficulty. They only rested when the procession was left behind or when Hannibal ordered a halt. All eight of them were tall men who didn't look old in the distance. Hannibal was gradually overcoming his mistrust. They must want as much as we do to get the mountains behind them, he said to himself.

The road led through an inhospitable-looking landscape but one that lay completely open before us. There were no signs of fresh danger. The night was undisturbed. During the next two days the road became steeper. The great serpentine army moved more slowly but the mercenaries were in good spirits. They could see more and more of the mountains behind them. They were approaching the pass. In one and a half days, the guides promised. They asked Hannibal whether he thought it necessary that all eight of them should go as far as the pass, or whether three guides would not be enough. Hannibal saw that five of the old men were obviously exhausted. He gave them a reward that surprised them and let them go. He kept near him the three others who so far had not suffered from the road.

The army was feeling the effects of the climb. Every mercenary had to carry his marching-pack as well as his weapons. The baggage horses could not be overloaded, because here and there the roads were dangerously steep. At this height there were only a few isolated trees. One incautious step would start a fall of stones which swept down on its way with a roar. Then the mountain-sides answered with their thunder. Men and animals looked about them in alarm; they saw the terrible wilderness which surrounded them and pushed on because there was no choice for them.

The next day, the eighth of the climb, they saw the pass clearly in front of them. A ravine, the floor of which was hidden in its black depths, led up to it. The ravine was a narrow one; it mounted steadily up to the pass. It was divided in the middle by a gigantic rock which almost took up its whole width. The guides declared that there was a road on either side of the bare rock. Hannibal divided his army into two and ordered each half to advance along one side of the rock so that, if possible on that day, the whole procession might reach the saddle of the pass which led to Italy. The guides assured him that there was room for the whole army on the saddle. The sun shone down on to the pass while horsemen, mercenaries, elephants, and baggage-train entered the ravine. Hannibal covered the rear of the procession with the slingers. The elephants who were once more in the middle of the procession were coming up to the rock which lay like a barrier across the ravine. Carthalo and I and all the others looked longingly up to the pass. Another three hours, said the guides. The joyous news spread quickly. The mercenaries took it as part of the day's work that the road on which they were travelling was precipitous. It crumbled under the steps of the elephants. Suru was again walking with the greatest caution. Carthalo and I walked in front of him. No driver was sitting on his animal.

A ridge of mountain towered almost perpendicularly above the ravine. Shadows like black cloths hung down from it.

Suddenly we heard cries from the heights above us. The mountains were roused by the cries and roared an accompaniment to them. Some of the elephants were so frightened that they began to run away. They didn't get far, because the road gave under the weight of their footsteps. The pack-horses also lost their foothold in their fright. So we suffered considerable losses simply because of the noise which assailed us.

Then again, as at the first attack, stones began to thunder down. We were penned up like sheep in the ravine. As there was no surface growth of grass on the slope, every falling stone loosened others and these turned into avalanches which made gaps in the procession and buried men and animals. There could now be no question of climbing the heights from which destruc-

124

tion had descended upon us. The old men had led us into a trap far more cunning than the first.

This time not only I crouched for shelter under Suru, but also Carthalo. Suru was strangely quiet. He picked his way so surely that it looked as if he knew exactly when and where the stones were going to roll down. We kept under his belly, as young elephants do when they feel endangered.

Suru stood still; a fragment of rock rolled down the length of an elephant ahead of him. He took two quicker steps; immediately behind him a fall of stones crashed down. It was as if the elephant were playing a game of which he knew each move beforehand. In this way he took about thirty steps forward. Then he came to an overhanging wall of rock. Now he stood still, pressing up against the grey rock as if he had grown together with it. Carthalo and I were crouching in safety under a rock from which warmth came.

We stared at each other open-mouthed. In the midst of this hell Suru had discovered a corner into which Death couldn't find his way.

Most of the army was without cover and so completely exposed to the incalculable fragments of rock which bounded down from the heights. A cluster of men had collected round Suru. Now and again those who stood outside the cluster were swept away.

And now a cry of horror echoed along the ravine: 'The devils are coming.' The men who had sent such a devastating attack ahead of them were now coming down themselves from the heights. They came boldly down walls of rock which seemed to offer no foothold. They all rushed towards one spot where so many stones had come down that every man and beast had perished. The mountain folk took possession of this heap of devastation which had only existed for the last hour or two. They had accomplished their aim, they had cut off Hannibal from his horse, his elephants, and from Monomach's mercenaries. Now they turned resolutely towards the rear-guard. Hannibal and his Berserkers flung themselves against them and beat the mountain folk back. Maharbal attacked them in the rear. For two hours the battle raged backwards and forwards. The ravine made it impossible to attack the aggressors in the flank and they were able to hold their position until it grew dark. When night fell both battles stopped. Hannibal was still cut off from his army. He made an attempt to break through after midnight, but he met with bitter resistance and was wounded. It was with difficulty that his men saved him from falling into the hands of the Allobroges. The decisive attack was postponed till the morning. When it grew light and when the Carthaginians advanced from both sides to break the barrier they found the pile of stones deserted. The mountain folk had fled during the late night hours. They could only have climbed up the almost perpendicular walls on both sides of the barricade. How they had done that in the dark and without noise no one who looked up at the face of the rock could explain. They had left an uncanny silence behind them. Fear took hold of the men who were faced with the deserted heap of stones. They searched the heights. Nothing moved there. A few birds began to fly noiselessly round in circles. They were gigantic birds, such as no one in the army had seen before. The morning remained quiet. The mountains kept silence as though it was not in them to roar when they were shouted at. Nothing could be heard but the groans of the wounded. The living, who had escaped with fear, avoided talking to one another as they had been used to do, in case one loudly spoken word might let loose the destruction again. Carthalo went off to find out how many elephants were still alive.

'Twenty,' he said when he came back. Everyone who heard this took it for a miracle.

The order came through to the Indos to set the elephants in motion. The disturbed animals picked their way over dead men and wreckage. Hannibal, who had gone forward to get an idea of the extent of the losses, ordered the elephants to be brought to the head of the procession. The whole way along, the mercenaries looked at the grey giants as if they were ghosts. I heard

127

them counting aloud. They had given the elephants up—now a whole twenty had come alive out of the ravine. And so all was not lost; the giants made that plain by their appearance. Hannibal inspected the elephants. He said a few words to each of them.

With the elephants the pack animals who carried the elephants' food had also been ordered to the front. Half of them were missing. Nevertheless Hannibal had a full ration given out and this did the pack animals good as well as the elephants. He was determined to get all the survivors to the pass. He wanted to get the army as quickly as possible out of the horrors which now surrounded them.

The sky was covered with cloud, but the pass could be seen by everyone. Now the elephants led the climb. Perhaps it was the sight of them that kept the Allobroges from attacking again, or else they considered that they had already wrought enough devastation.

I heard from Carthalo, who had been in the vanguard listening to conversations, that two of the three old men had escaped when the attack began. Monomach had had the third put to the torture in order to find out what had been the motive of their treachery. But the old man had suffered all the pangs of torture in silence, and at the end had looked as happy as if he had succeeded in escaping. 'There you have them,' Monomach had summed up bitterly; 'even in death they deceive you.'

In the end the old man had been as silent as snow, so Carthalo had heard.

21

IT grew noticeably darker and soon afterwards began to snow. The flakes that came down were small and felt dry. A light wind got up and made the flakes dance. The ground had already been frozen several times and so the snow didn't melt.

Soon every step left a mark and when Suru put his feet down he stamped enormous seals in the loose whiteness. The elephants were good pace-makers. They took their time. They climbed patiently—it wasn't necessary to urge them on. They marked out the way unmistakably for those behind them.

The wind grew stronger. It blew thicker veils of snow against the procession. No one could now see more than ten footsteps ahead. Eyes and faces began to smart. The path grew slippery. More and more often someone fell. Knees were bleeding and jerkins became caked with frozen snow when men fell their length and slipped along a little way. Tools and weapons were lost, also pack animals with their loads. The light blanket of snow was deceptive; it made the slope seem steeper than it was. Every step was a risk. The elephants too were using their last stocks of energy. Suddenly the Dwarf fell—we all heard his driver's shriek. It wasn't possible to rush to his help. Everyone had to see to it that he kept his own foot-hold. It was impossible to see anything because of the driving snow, but the news soon came along. The Giant had tried to hold his elephant; the elephant had rolled over him. Only nineteen now. . . . Suru was feeling with his trunk for possible foot-holds. Sometimes he lifted his trunk up towards the pass which had hidden itself from us. Now it was the mountains that rejected us. They caused us losses without doing anything. It no longer needed falling rocks to make gaps in Hannibal's procession. The mountains were against us and the sky which was spread out over them was our enemy. It threw wind on to us and snow which grew murderous as soon as it combined with the mountains. It took longer and longer for those who fell to stand up again. Some lay still where they fell and no longer wanted to be helped. The mountains had defeated them. Without a single movement they smote the evil-doer who had disturbed their solitude with the noise of arms. The rocks had awakened from the sleep of ages. Fear crept into our hearts.

'We shall soon have got him, this accursed pass,' panted Hannibal. He was leading the procession and carrying his own pack

129

and weapons like the lowest of his mercenaries. When a driver's cries betrayed the fact that an elephant had come to a standstill, Hannibal was soon at the exhausted elephant's side. He talked to him until he went on again. We all knew that we should be lost if night overtook the army on this steep slope. Hannibal made circles round the elephants like a dog round his herd. On one of these circles he came upon me lying on the ground and hanging on to the slope by my hands. He knelt down beside me and tried to lift me up. 'Let go,' he said; 'I've got you.'

My face was turned to the ground. 'I can't go on,' I whispered. 'You're wrong,' I heard him say; 'you can go on, my little Carthaginian!' He took me by the shoulders and turned me round. I looked him in the face; he tried to smile, but even he couldn't do that. Then I stood up. And now I stayed at his side, and it wasn't necessary for him to hold me.

And then suddenly the road wasn't steep any longer. Hannibal reconnoitred a little way ahead along the level ground. He came back and roared down the slope, 'The pass! We've got it!'

The cry was passed on and Hannibal listened to it. It was repeated many times.

'Do you hear?' he panted. 'All those haven't given up.' He pressed me to him in a wild exultation. 'We and the elephants were the first!'

We had reached the pass. It was a large saddle; that we could see even in the snow. One elephant after another moved past Hannibal. The animals put their feet down in surprise, as though they couldn't understand that there was still a road in the world that wasn't steep.

On the pass Tembo collapsed with exhaustion. Suru and another elephant knelt down by his flanks and went on pressing and pushing them until they had prised him on to his feet again. Then Suru found a protected spot and the elephants collected round him. There were nineteen of them—except for the Dwarf they had all managed it.

The anger of the sky calmed down. It was certainly still snowing but the snow was no longer driven; it was falling silently.

130

The wind had stopped. The elephants stood closely pressed together in order to warm one another, and we kept close to them because warmth went out from them. We made a fire immediately beside them. The elephants accepted it. The drivers squatted round the fire in thick clusters. When the pack animals arrived the elephants were covered with the large red blankets which were part of their war equipment. They were also fed.

The ration for each elephant was now no longer a large one. We ate and for us there was enough. The fire thawed us.

Here and there fires were burning in the snow. The pass led away level towards the south and afforded plenty of room for those of us who were still left.

Carthalo was sitting by me. He had wrapped me in a pelt. 'You behaved like Hannibal,' he whispered in my ear. He also spoke of Suru and the other elephants in terms of high praise.

'And there are people who call them Lucanian oxen,' he said indignantly. I looked at him without understanding.

'The Romans, who else?' he said scornfully. 'Because they met their first elephants in Lucania they call them Lucanian oxen. Oxen!' Carthalo said angrily. 'I must apologize to Suru for their impudence.' He stood up and walked towards the elephants as though his plan couldn't be postponed. But by now I couldn't stand up, and I drew the blanket closer round me. It was still snowing. In this whiteness which came down silently the fires stood out like little suns in the mist. I looked towards the fires, until fires and snow melted into one another before my eyes.

22

WHEN I woke up I felt warm. I put it down to the pelt into which I had crept in my sleep. While I slipped out of it the sun was shining on to my face. Around me everyone had been up and active for a long time.

'You must be one of the Seven Sleepers,' Carthalo said teasingly; 'it's nearly midday; aren't you hungry?'

Carthalo gave me some food.

'You've already missed something,' he said. 'We were all buried. Thousands of little white mounds—one of us under each. And you're the last to get up!' He pulled me up. 'We had nineteen white elephants. The elephants—the whole army—under one blanket! The sun drew it off us and has fetched out the mountains. Look about you!'

I blinked. The hard light cut into my eyes. I had to get used to the sun first. It was strong and high in the sky. I was amazed to see what it had done in a few hours.

When night had fallen, everything about me had been a cold wilderness, a cheerless end of the world. Now the giant mountains were standing there, silver against the blue of the sky, an unending chain, glittering, as though they were new-born that day. One peak towered up behind the other. Now and again its sparkle made a peak dance, like a star in extreme cold. They seemed to be made of ice, but the wonderful thing was that warmth came to us from them. The white peaks helped the sun to warm the world.

But where was the world, the world in which people lived? My eyes fell on a soft blanket which spread itself out beneath us, and which seemed to have no beginning and no end. It looked as if glaciers had flowed down from all the peaks and met together in a white sea which was hovering high above the world.

'We're above the clouds,' Carthalo announced. He was in a good humour. I looked round for Suru. Where the elephants had collected round Suru there were now none to be seen. They were standing about either alone or in small groups. Suru I saw nowhere.

'Where's Suru?'

'He'll be back soon,' Carthalo assured me. 'He's looking for water like everyone else.'

I set out along the road and soon found Suru. He was standing aside from the bustle of the camp at a spot where the melting snow had tunnelled a ditch. He looked as though he would never tire of sucking the water up and then squirting it on to himself, particularly on to his legs which were obviously hurting him. Suru looked thinner; his flanks were hollow. I had a piece of bread in my pocket and I gave it to him. He took it greedily.

'Have the elephants been fed yet?' I asked Carthalo when I had got back to him.

133

'Suru and I have shared my breakfast.'

'Is there no fodder left?'

'Down there,' Carthalo assured me, 'under that blanket of cloud. The day after tomorrow there will be enough for everyone to eat; the day after tomorrow we go down.'

'Why not today?' I asked in alarm. 'Are the elephants to starve?'

'You oughtn't only to consider the elephants,' Carthalo admonished me; 'there are the men too.'

The mercenaries were in a bad way. Many of them weren't capable of going on with the march. Hannibal had ordered a rest-camp for two days. He was counting on the sun. As there was enough for the men to eat, the quickest way to help them to renew their strength would be to leave them in peace. There was no fear of an attack up here.

Hannibal also wanted to reorganize the army after its terrible losses. As it had been with Mago's three hundred after his skirmish with the Romans, so it was now on a large scale. Almost every other man had fallen. It is true that some stragglers appeared, who had been encouraged by the sun to finish the climb to the pass by themselves, and a few horses, injured by their falls, turned up at the camp in the course of the day. But that could blind no one to the fact that the army had melted down to nearly half its size. Seventeen thousand mercenaries and more than two thousand horsemen had perished during the nine days since the crossing of the mountain torrent.

The next day the blanket of cloud which had hidden the valleys and plains began to disperse, and in the course of an hour it disappeared completely in the south. To the north of the pass it was still there and so the ravines were still hidden from us. We could see the whole country southwards to the Po. The great river lay there in the distance like a shining thread. The mercenaries looked down on to the plain spellbound. Even the wounded who had dragged themselves as far as the pass roused themselves and stood up. Hannibal climbed on to a rock so that everyone could see him. He looked for a long time towards the south. Then he turned to the army.

'There lies Rome!' he cried to the mercenaries, holding out an arm towards Italy. 'We are standing on its outermost walls. Soon we shall go down to meet those who are waiting for us. Through treachery our army has dwindled in the mountains—on the plains it will grow again and be stronger than ever. The worst is behind you. Now only victories await you. Our friends are down there, and behind them the enemy whom we shall sweep off the earth in fewer battles than there are fingers on one of my hands. Then there will be nothing more in our way till we knock on the gates of Rome. For you who have climbed over walls which reach almost up to the sky, the city wall of Rome will be no obstacle. You who have conquered the Alps shall have Rome as your prize. Take the city! I bequeath it to you! Look behind you! There lies Death. You have humbled him; he doesn't dare to show you his face. And now look at the south! There lies Life. It is waiting for you.'

When Hannibal stopped speaking there were no shouts of acclamation. We had listened to his words with our necks craned. He climbed down from the rock and went up to a wounded man who was leaning on his spear.

'We were in Hell together,' he said loudly enough to be heard by many others. 'Now we're going to take our reward for having drawn the Devil's teeth.'

Hannibal's speech had driven away our gloomy thoughts. We were feverishly waiting for the descent, for the friends on that side of the mountains—and for the enemy. Fires were lighted on the pass for the last time. What was left of our supplies of food was shared, each one trying to outbid the other. Carthalo offered food to Silenos. 'We are all brothers now,' he declared solemnly; 'we became brothers in Hell.' Carthalo's face was burning. When he began to make a speech to me I saw that he was feverish.

The pass was turned into a vast banqueting-table, at which there was wild merry-making. We were intoxicated without having drunk.

23

WHEN night fell silence spread over the camp. It grew colder. Carthalo wrapped himself and me in a pelt and two blankets, and so we could keep each other warm.

'The elephants do the same,' he reminded me. He was growing hotter. We were lying not far from the elephants.

'For them too the hardest part is over,' he assured me. 'Better days are coming for us all.'

We were lying and looking out into the night. It was full of glittering stars. Round us the ice was sparkling and in the ice we could see the stars again. I could feel on my face that the cold was beginning to bite. But I wasn't cold. Lying beside Carthalo was like lying beside a stove that is throwing out heat. It was the fever burning in him. Sometimes he lay so still that I could hear the quick beats of his heart. Whenever he said anything I saw his breath white over his face.

'There are only two more steps to take,' he said suddenly, 'down to Rome, and then home to Carthage, to my town, to your town, my little Carthaginian!'

He turned to me and said with his hot breath, 'What would the coast of Africa be without Carthage!' He raised himself a little and looked towards the wide dark gap in the south which was the opening between the mountains. 'There it is, there the town is shining,' he whispered in great excitement. 'Can you see the yellow coast and the white stone ship by it? That is Carthage, master of all the western seas. It lies for ever at anchor off the coast of Africa.'

I too propped myself on my elbow, but I could only see icy peaks and glittering stars.

Carthalo was still talking. I shut my eyes, and now I could see the white stone ship under the blue sky of Africa. I saw the harbours about which he was talking, the outer one for trading ships, the inner one for war. In the middle of the naval harbour I

136

saw the little island with the commandant's tower—and the ships coming to land in between the decorated pillars.

'Where else are there such walls?' Carthalo said ecstatically. 'There is room within them for three hundred elephants, six thousand horses, and twenty thousand mercenaries! Above the walls the *Byrsa*, the castle, towering up, and between harbour and castle the town, its steep narrow streets full of noise and dirt and crowds, its busy markets, its dwelling-houses swarming with life, cutting off the sea and sky from one another.'

In his fever Carthalo began to talk to sailors in red jackets, to traders in dye who brought their cloth to the market, purple, red-brown, dark crimson cloths—wherever he went he came across old acquaintances. He patted donkeys on the neck as they came from the well of the thousand pitchers, the only well in the town, each donkey with pointed jugs full of fresh water in its panniers, attended by boys whose business it had been from the eighth year of their life to take the donkeys to fetch water from the well.

And then Carthalo got angry. 'Those street boys!' he muttered in a scolding tone. 'Do you see the man in the short tunic with ear ornaments, after whom the boys are calling *Gugga*, little rat! He is one of the dealers who use aged slaves to carry job lots to market. He'll grow rich because he's saving. His father saved money, he himself is a mean man—but his son will be one of those who sleep on the money chest and own a country house out at Megara, in the midst of gardens and vineyards, between the mountains and the sea, where Barca was born and where Hannibal first saw the light. Look at the trees, how laden they are with fruit, how fertile the fields are, right up to the desert, and look at the trenches that have been dug between the fields and the desert—as if between two enemies, so that the desert cannot fall upon Carthage! Everywhere there is life, and that is just what a Carthaginian likes. There is life also in the peasants' huts which smell of cabbage and garlic, life in the dwelling-houses in which the have-nots sleep on cement floors, red with brick dust. All these celebrate the feast days as they come along,

137

they make a paste of flour and cheese and honey and eggs—they are all pastry-eaters, rich and poor, young and old; even in the back yards there is festive merry-making on holidays. Glass-blowers, and carpenters, sailors and peasants, rich merchants and little rats—there is life in them all, and they don't want to be anything else but what they are: Carthaginians. And only the slaves who work in the stone quarries on the coast, condemned to live in caves, with the ships that guard them always before them—only the slaves curse the life that doesn't belong to them any more. That will be the fate of all the Romans. We will beat them down until a slave slips out of the skin of every Roman. But we'—he drew me close up to him, shaking with fever—'we shall live happily ever afterwards. Carthage, we are on our way to you! The ice cannot hurt us because you keep us warm, you white stone ship which will never sink!'

He pressed my face up against his own rough, scarred, burning face. Then he looked at me out of eyes that shone in the darkness. 'We shall be happy there, you and Suru and I—there will be no ice, no snow, no Romans any more. Go to sleep now, little Carthalo, tomorrow we go down from the mountains to put an end to Rome.'

His hot hands let me go. He fell back exhausted. I was cold and crept farther into the pelt.

The next morning Carthalo woke me while the sky was still grey. Everyone was hurriedly throwing off blankets and snow to get ready for the descent. The sky was hanging so low that it touched the mountain-tops. It must have been snowing for some time, and it didn't look as if it was about to stop. But no one took this snow seriously any longer. We had seen the green valleys, they were drawing us to them, and we were confident that we would leave the snow behind us that day.

Carthalo was still feverish, but he wouldn't admit it. We walked beside the elephants, who had been glad to set out because their hunger was driving them. Never before had they been so near starvation. Hannibal put them at the head of the procession. The skin on their flanks hung loosely. But they

138

found the path under the snow more surely than either horse or man. As long as it was possible to descend by widely sweeping serpentine roads there was no rest. When the road grew steeper even some of the elephants fell. Under the layer of newly fallen snow lay last year's snow and it had formed a crust or turned into ice. Under the feet of so many animals and men the fresh snow had turned into mush. In places it was only possible to move forward on our knees. Besides all this the driving snow blotted out the view. But the elephants were not to be beaten. They met the cunning of the mountains with a cunning of their own. Where the path turned into a steep icy slope they solved the problem by sitting down and then going cautiously into a slide, stretching out their forelegs in front of them to act as brakes. But the pack-horses' sharp hoofs went through the treacherous surface and were caught as in a pincer trap.

In those cases it was impossible to help. We cursed the mountain which was snapping at us with its icy jaws. At a place which no one would have thought unsafe one elephant fell over the edge of the path and perished.

The snow lasted about three more hours and then the sky broke through. We drew deep breaths of relief.

But suddenly a white precipice loomed up like a fortress. The path that led past this rock had been swept away by a landslide. We stared at the white wall that had sprung up in front of us and that towered above the steep slope. The slope was covered with stones for a thousand feet down from us. Hannibal looked farther up for a way of getting round this precipice and rock, but there was no way.

'If there is no path we will make one,' said Hannibal. No one understood what he meant. But he ordered the few trees that stood about like forgotten sentinels to be felled and then sawn into logs. The logs were piled up on one another against the rock. Soon they were on fire. An enormous flame licked up the face of the rock. The white stone turned black. When it was hot enough to crack Hannibal ordered it to be washed all over with melted snow. Vinegar was then squirted on to it. Now crevices began to show themselves in the face of the rock. All through the night Hannibal assaulted the white stone with fire and ice-water and vinegar. He made it soft and the stone began to yield. When morning came a narrow passage was chiselled in the white wall. Sappers were able to squeeze themselves through and then build a path above the abyss with tree trunks. They bridged the place that the landslide had made unsafe.

On the thirteenth day, when the sun was in the south, the path was ready. One elephant after another, one horse after another, one man after another walked along the path which in places was only a few feet wide. The elephants were the least afraid or all. Nevertheless one of them was lost when a tree trunk came untied. A new trunk was put in its place and more firmly fastened than the old one. A few horses who took fright were lost to the abyss but not a single man.

None of us had shut our eyes during the night. We had all been collecting wood to feed the fire, sweeping the snow into piles, melting it in cauldrons, and with fire and water we had driven Death out of the white rock. But now we were all little more than ghosts. The elephants marched silently into the valley like enormous phantoms.

The air grew warmer. We began to stumble over roots and found ourselves walking over tufts of grass. We looked at one another furtively but took good care not to say anything; we were afraid that the first spoken word might wake us out of a dream. As soon as the land made a rest possible Hannibal ordered a halt. Many of us dropped down where we were and fell asleep.

'What beautiful trees!' I heard Carthalo say. I saw Suru making for the trees. When the clamour of the elephants' meal began I was already half asleep. Carthalo bent over me.

'Seventeen have come through,' he said, and his face looked as if the war was over and won.

24

On the second day of the descent we marched through the territory of the Salassi. Magal had talked of them on the 'island'. He had said: 'You will come first to the land of the Salassi who are your friends.'

The Salassi, who showed themselves by the side of our road, didn't behave like friends or like enemies—they didn't know how to behave. They seemed surprised and embarrassed, and their children were frightened at the sight of us and ran away. The Salassi had been expecting an army; here were clusters of ragged figures, several of whom were even without weapons. Half-starving men with faces that had grown savage were dragging themselves down into the valley. We were like beaten men and could hardly stand upright on our feet. Even the terrifying grey beasts who led the procession were walking so unsteadily that it looked as if they might fall at any moment. Many of us were wounded and as pale as death, and the horrors we had been through were reflected in our eyes. Can these men be conquerors? Can they be invincible? The Salassi had seen Roman armies. They knew that Rome had already dispatched legions to fight against Hannibal. And did these shadows of soldiers think they could lay Rome low?

The Salassi gave Hannibal's men what they wanted, but they gave it as if they were feeding beggars. They kept their houses open but they stood in the door-ways, they didn't go out to meet the new-comers—and no one dreamed of coming with us. The utmost they would do was to barter their weapons with us. Most of them watched as from a distance and kept silence, telling us by their manner that they didn't want to have anything to do with their deliverers.

That day we reached the edge of the plain. The descent had only taken two days; we had met with no opposition, there had been no ambushes lying in wait for us, no hostile agitation—but with every step we took we had met pity, and that was far worse than enmity. The mercenaries felt it a disgrace to be exposed to pitying looks. Carthalo too was depressed. He tried to hide it from me, but I could see that disappointment was gnawing at him. His fever had returned and was even higher than before, but he wouldn't hear of sparing himself.

On the banks of a little river Hannibal ordered a halt. The elephants waded into the water although it was cold. Suru stayed longer than the others in the river. He was cooling his breast with the water all the time. Carthalo noticed this and when at last Suru climbed out on to the bank he examined him.

'He has a fever,' he said anxiously, 'he must be in pain.' And then Carthalo discovered the source of the fever. On his breast where it joined his neck there was a swelling. A large abscess was hidden under the folds of his skin. Carthalo blamed himself for not having noticed it before. 'It must have been hurting him for days.' He felt in his pockets, took out bread and the remnants of a lump of salt and gave Suru the tit-bits. Then he took hold of his trunk and rubbed his face on it, at the same time talking to me. He then told me to go away. When after walking ten steps I turned round, I saw Carthalo thrusting his dagger into Suru's breast and then leaping away to the side. Suru was frightened; his trunk sprang up, and out of his breast, the skin of which was stretched tight, a spurt of blood shot up. Nothing more happened. Suru didn't even turn round to Carthalo who was cleaning his dagger with soil.

'They have great powers of endurance,' said Carthalo that evening to me, 'and they always know when people are trying to help them.'

I was still trembling with fright. I admitted that I had been afraid for a moment that Carthalo's dagger might have pierced Suru's heart.

'His heart is very deep-seated,' Carthalo said reassuringly.

Once every hour we examined Suru. He let Carthalo go up to him. The wound was the size of an open hand, but the pain seemed to be over.

143

The next morning we found that Suru had covered up the wound with a plaster of clay. Carthalo seemed to have got over his fever. He no longer looked dejected. 'Victory is in the air,' he maintained, when the order came to start.

I looked at the mercenaries. They were as ragged and emaciated as ever, and I was surprised by what Carthalo had said.

On that day we were met by ambassadors from Magal. They were the horsemen who had crossed the Alps with him. Hannibal asked why Magal hadn't come himself. He was busy, the horsemen explained. He was besieging the town of the Taurini for the reason that the Taurini had spoken disparagingly of the 'Alp-stormers'.

'Of you?' asked Hannibal.

'Of you!' Magal's men retorted indignantly. 'They call you "the men who have come down".'

Hannibal's face darkened. 'They shall make our acquaintance,' he promised. 'How far is it to their town?'

'Two days.'

'Are they have-nots?'

'They have everything that they want.'

'So much the better.'

Hannibal sent the horsemen back to Magal with the message that he was to postpone the storming of the town till he arrived with the Carthaginian army. He claimed the town as booty for 'the men who have come down'.

Carthalo's face brightened when he heard of the Taurini's impudence. Throughout the army the desire awoke to come to grips with men who had a town to lose. The enemy who had presented himself so unexpectedly had made an army out of a multitude of ghosts. There was even a change in the elephants. The nearer they came to the town of the Taurini, the more threatening they looked. Celtic warriors, infected by the mercenaries' lust for battle, joined us. Weapons, horses, and wagons were offered to us. The wounded men no longer wanted to be left behind. Rumours of the riches of the town of the Taurini were heard on all sides.

144

Three days later the town was taken at the first blow. The Taurini, paralysed by the sight of the war elephants, were no match for the savagery of Hannibal's army. Hannibal left the plundering of the town to his mercenaries. He spared the lives of a hundred of the prisoners and drove them all together into a pen. The army was drunk with the sudden victory. And now what Hannibal had foretold on the pass came true. The gaps which the stone avalanches had made in the mountains were filled. Detachments of armed men came from every direction to join the army. Magal with a large and handsome escort was the first to arrive. Insubres came and Boii from a long distance, even some Salassi, and this time they were not offended by the rags of the victors. Moreover the rags were now disappearing. The mercenaries were wearing the clothes they had taken as booty. There were also enough weapons—all that was necessary was to take them from the hands of the slain men. There were horses and saddles, wine and plenty to eat. Flocks of black birds fell from the skies and in like manner slave-traders appeared in hordes to buy the surviving women and children. Suddenly the pockets of the mercenaries began to bulge. The war was now in full spate and was taking the course they had expected.

I watched all this from a distance, from the elephants' resting-place, chosen by Hannibal so that they might be away from the riotous behaviour in the camp. When the town was stormed the elephants were only taken up to the walls—that had caused enough terror. Not a single elephant had entered the town, even after the battle. Hannibal was anxious to spare the seventeen surviving elephants as much as possible. Far away from the camp, where Baleares and Insubres, Numidians and Boii, Spartans and Salassi, were fraternizing so noisily, the elephants and their drivers were by themselves for a few days. Every morning Suru led his reduced herd down to the river. The sun sparkled on their broad wet backs. The elephants were watched from a respectful distance by the natives of the district. Day by day the children ventured a little nearer. For a week it looked as if the elephants had nothing to do with the war. But anyone with an

145

understanding eye couldn't fail to see that they were full of unrest. They collected by the river for long consultations. We heard their rumbling conversation flowing and ebbing. Carthalo, who like the rest of us was lying in the sun, listened to them with half an ear. For him there was no doubt as to what they were talking about. 'First they will talk about the past,' he explained to me. 'You wouldn't believe how proud they are that they've accomplished it all: ravines, mountain rivers, the pass, that accursed white rock! They remember every single step.' Carthalo assured me that no human being has as good a memory as an elephant. He listened more carefully to the sound coming from the river. 'Now they are talking about what lies before them,' he told me. 'They can smell the Romans from a distance; they catch the scent of them long before we do. They will show the Romans what seventeen elephants are worth.'

A week later some of the armed mercenaries crossed to the other bank. Sentinels were posted all round the camp.

'It smells of Romans,' said Carthalo, when the command came to lead the elephants into the camp in full battle array.

Hannibal told us to parade the elephants in the open space in the middle of the camp. He climbed on to Suru in order to speak to the army. The mercenaries and auxiliaries looked up at him with eager faces. During the last few hours rumours had been going round: 'The Romans are advancing. . . .'

The spies whom Hannibal had sent out had come back, and some deserters also presented themselves in the camp. It was the same Scipio who had wanted to engage the Carthaginians by the Rhône; now he was determined to bring Hannibal to a halt at the foot of the Alps—he had already thrown a bridge over the Po. Hannibal confirmed the rumours.

'As for the Romans, I will tell you all that there is to be told,' he cried to the mercenaries. 'Men have come to us who up till now have sided with the Romans. Scipio has done what he could to set their blood on fire. What he has achieved you can see: they have run away from him. And no wonder! Listen to what he told them!' Hannibal now let some of the deserters speak. He himself translated Scipio's speech. He had the laugh on his side at once when he addressed his men as Romans. '"Romans!"' he translated with exaggerated gestures, '"I am sorry to tell you that yours will be only half a victory, for you will be fighting against an enemy who is already defeated—by the mountains, over which that madman who calls himself Hannibal drove his mercenaries. You will be fighting against starving men, against shadows of men, whose shoulders and heads have been galled by the rocks, whose fingers and toes are frost-bitten, whose joints are numbed."'

Laughter broke out round Hannibal, for he examined his hands challengingly, and many of his listeners did the same and shook their heads. A week ago these words would have been true; now they sounded ridiculous. And when Hannibal went on to speak of broken weapons, lamed horses, and of an army that had dwindled away to a fraction of its former size, the unrestrained merriment of the mercenaries who were satiated with booty and drunk with victory broke out into riotous noise.

'"Romans!"' cried Hannibal. '"You will be faced with beaten men, and you will have nothing to do but give them the death-blow. Give these upstarts the punishment due to them; they owe you tribute. Treat them as though they were rebellious slaves. And this frantic young man, who forced this war upon us, shall be cast into chains as he deserves!" He means me,' Hannibal concluded and the mercenaries again broke out into an uproar. They demanded turbulently to be allowed to advance against the Romans.

'Do not underestimate them,' Hannibal said, and now he was serious. 'They know what they are fighting for. They are fighting for their city, their houses, their fields, their cattle, their mothers, and their brothers. If they are not the victors they will be slaves. For them everything is at stake—for the first time. For us too! Don't deceive yourselves, there will be no escape. We have the mountains behind us and the sea on both sides of us—and not a single ship at hand to rescue us. We have only

ourselves. But is that not enough? You know me; I have grown up in your midst. Every one of you has seen how I deal with an enemy. And I know you—each one of you, and know the value I set on you. War has turned us from boys into men, we're in

148

our element in war as fishes are in water, as birds are in the air. Our opponents will be new to the work, hastily picked and inexperienced. This Scipio is only half a year old as a general—as a leader he is like a child who hasn't yet learnt to walk. And a man like that calls us his slaves! The Romans—this I promise you—shall be *your* slaves; each of you shall have two Romans as slaves. They demanded that we should be delivered up to them as criminals; torture and death was to be our lot. It will be *their* lot. You shall inherit their fields and their gardens, their houses and their possessions. And they will be left with nothing, you with everything.'

The mercenaries and auxiliaries greeted Hannibal's words with unrestrained applause. The elephants grew uneasy. Hannibal ordered us to take them away. So I didn't see what happened next in the open space. In order to fan the flame of the mercenaries' lust for battle Hannibal ordered the hundred captive Taurini to be brought into the camp. They were given permission to fight for their lives. They were mostly young men and they greedily accepted the offer. Some of them showed by wild dance steps their readiness to fight to the finish in single combat. That Taurini would be fighting Taurini did not deter them. They were supplied with weapons and Hannibal presented the victors with a horse. A loud roar announced the end of each fight. Carthalo who had watched some of the fights came away from the camp with a crimson face. It seemed as if he would never stop praising the bravery of these men who were doomed to die. 'The survivors will now fight on our side,' he announced proudly. 'Who but Hannibal could accomplish this? Out of yesterday's enemies to make allies, out of Boii, Insubres, Salassi and Taurini to make Carthaginians, out of a disheartened mob to make an army? And this Roman rabble dares . . .' He ended in incoherent attacks upon Scipio and his like; he accused the Romans of every imaginable baseness and prophesied their immediate doom.

An impatience that he couldn't shake off had taken possession of him. Carthage was drawing him. When the nights came on his face began to burn. There were deep shadows under his eyes. I was anxious about him and told Silenos of my anxiety. Silenos arranged that Synhal should examine him. Synhal gave Carthalo an ointment to be rubbed on to his chest and back. When I

150

rubbed his back I heard his breath rattling. More and more often I heard him say, 'Sweep the Romans into the sea! Home to Carthage!'

25

HANNIBAL moved along the Ticino towards the Po. The days were still warm, although winter was at the door. The sun invigorated both men and animals; the mercenaries could hardly wait to come face to face with the enemy. On the third day after the departure from the town of the Taurini Hannibal moved the army into a fortified camp. It made him uneasy that he had not yet come upon Scipio's legions. The country was not open; he was afraid of falling into a trap. The next morning he moved out with the horse troops on a wide front to find the enemy. Woods were combed, ravines scoured, hills scanned. The day grew hot. The horses' hoofs threw up clouds of dust.

Hannibal rode up to the top of a range of hills with Maharbal, Mago and a small retinue. What he saw from there took his breath away. He had the Roman horse troops before him. Like Hannibal, Scipio was looking for the enemy, and he also was riding at the head of about three thousand horse. He also was taking up his position on the range of hills.

Hannibal was there first and now he advanced against the Romans without a moment's delay. Maharbal and Mago spread out the two wings of the horse troops. Under cover of the hills the Numidians reached the flanks of the Romans. The collision of the two fronts was so violent that many of the riders were flung from their saddles. They fought on grimly on foot. Wounded horses wrought confusion; in a short time the field was covered with dead and wounded. The battle surged backwards and forwards. Now Maharbal and Mago broke into the flanks of the Romans with their Numidians and after that there was no more organized resistance. Each man fought for his own

151

life. Scipio too fought desperately. The tumult was greatest round him. He was struck down from his horse. Hannibal saw it and tried to seize the Consul, but he couldn't break his way through to him. Without a thought for their own lives the Roman horsemen barred the way to the place where their general lay under the hoofs of his horse. Before Hannibal's eyes a young horseman fought his way through to the wounded Consul, set him on his horse, and then he and the other encircled Romans fought their way with much bloodshed out of the turmoil. They broke down whatever resistance they met and shook off their pursuers. Hundreds sacrificed themselves to help this one man to escape. Hundreds of panicking horses were galloping about with empty saddles. The attack of the Numidians had broken the ranks of the Romans and made it possible for the Carthaginians to mow them down. Hannibal had not lost half as many horsemen as the Romans. During the pursuit he pushed on as far as a range of hills from which he had a view of the Roman camp. It was a half-day's march from the Carthaginian camp.

Hannibal turned back. He was determined to attack the camp the next day and to force the Romans to a decisive battle. He rode into his own camp with hundreds of captured horses. The mercenaries envied the horsemen their victory. They felt they had been robbed of something and were only comforted by the thought of the imminent battle. 'Tomorrow will be the end of the Romans,' Carthalo assured Suru and me with a light in his eyes.

That night he didn't sleep, as I could tell by his face the next morning. It was as grey as ashes. Suru was standing in full battle array earlier than all the other elephants. As Carthalo buckled on Suru's breast-plate he apologized to him: 'I shan't be able to help you; today is the great day. When it is over there will be no more Roman legions.' Suru submitted patiently to the putting on of his armour. His wound was healed.

Hannibal moved his army out of camp in an order in which they could go into battle at any time. The horse troops had the order to protect our flanks. Hannibal planned to make the elephants and the horse bear the brunt of the battle. Their superiority had proved itself at the first engagement. Hannibal reckoned that Scipio wouldn't wait for the attack in the camp, but that he would draw up his legions on the open field in readiness for the Carthaginians. With his feelers well out Hannibal began to march towards the south.

The enemy seemed nowhere, neither on the hills behind which the Roman camp lay hidden, nor on the field outside the camp. There was no sign of life in the camp and no guards at the entries; the trenches were not occupied. Scipio had moved out during the night.

When Carthalo looked down at the deserted camp he uttered an oath that I had never before heard on his lips. 'Do they mean us to run after them until we have no feet to run with?' he said angrily, looking at me with a flicker in his eyes. He felt deceived.

Hannibal sent out Maharbal and Mago with a thousand horse to get on the track of the enemy. He told us to take off the elephants' coverings and armour. It seemed from all his orders that he wasn't reckoning on an early battle.

By the end of that day Carthalo was raging so violently against the Romans that Synhal advised him most urgently not to give himself up to his anger. 'It eats up too much of you,' he warned Carthalo. He brewed a hot drink for him. The rattling of his breath and the curses both abated. Once he actually laughed. When Maharbal and Mago came back with their horsemen the report went quickly round the camp that about six hundred Romans had fallen into the hands of the Carthaginians. They had been breaking down the bridge of boats across the Po over which Scipio's legions had withdrawn, and they had taken a little too much time over it. Our horsemen had not been able to take the bridge itself. From the prisoners they had learnt that Scipio was badly wounded. It was also said that the youthful horseman, who had set Scipio on his horse and led him out of the danger zone, was Scipio's son.

The next day the army moved up to the Po. The Romans had burnt all the boats and barges on the opposite bank. There was

153

nothing to be done but to find a place farther upstream where the river was shallower. When that was found Hannibal ordered a dam to be built to break the force of the current. He built it with the elephants. One elephant stood behind the other; the animals, led by Suru, went willingly into the water and then stood still, half turned against the current. Then the mercenaries and the horses crossed in the calmer water, swimming or wading, holding on to their bags of hide. Men and horses dried themselves by fires. Hannibal ordered tents to be set up. The war seemed to have moved away into the far distance. Mercenaries and horsemen gave themselves up to sleep without any thought of danger, and I saw drivers sleeping by the fires. But Carthalo was restless.

He wanted us to spend the night with Suru and so we lay down in the midst of the elephants. I listened to Carthalo's breathing. He grew calmer but he didn't sleep. The elephants didn't go to sleep quickly either, although they were standing quite still. For a long time they kept their ears in the position in which they could catch any sound. Not till nearly midnight did they feel safe enough to give up listening. And now Carthalo grew quieter. Above me I saw a dark path which led through the midst of the stars. It was Suru's trunk. I looked at it till I fell asleep.

26

THROUGH his spies Hannibal learnt that Scipio had moved with his legions into a camp near the town of Placentia. Hannibal was determined to bring his enemy to bay, or at least to drive him before him—he would not leave him in peace any longer. So he dispatched Maharbal with his horse to harry him. Maharbal succeeded in cutting off some of the cohorts from the Roman camp. Hannibal set up his own camp immediately beneath the walls o the town, challengingly near the Roman entrenchments. But Scipio avoided a battle. He was still suffering from the wound he had had on the Ticino and he was waiting for reinforcements. His hesitation affected the legions, particularly the Italian auxiliary troops in his camp. One night the guards at the camp gates were surprised, and two thousand mercenaries and two hundred horsemen broke out. The Romans who tried to prevent this treacherous sally were cut down. The Carthaginians received the deserters with open arms. Hannibal sent them to their homes. There they were to make recruits and each man was to come back with ten others to fight with Hannibal for freedom from the Roman yoke. There were still some Celts in the immediate neighbourhood waiting to see what was going to happen. Hannibal urged them to come on to his side. When they made excuses he pressed them harder. A few of their settlements went up in flames. The raids of the Numidians who fell upon the terrified inhabitants left devastated tracts of land behind them. Those who escaped with their lives accepted their fate and went over to the Carthaginians. It was clear that there was no help to be expected from the Romans—they had enough to do to defend themselves.

These enforced allies shared the Carthaginian provisions, but Hannibal's men were themselves far from lavishly supplied, and he had to put his mercenaries temporarily on half rations. But a lucky stroke put an end to this difficulty. By means of agents he had made contact with the commandant of the Roman town Clastidium, and the commandant allowed himself to be bribed. For the small sum of four hundred gold pieces he sold the town to the Carthaginians. Now their hunger was at an end. The town granaries were full. Hannibal allowed the garrison and the citizens free withdrawal.

The days grew noticeably shorter. In the evenings mist rose

from the Po and the Trebia and then the land disappeared and was hidden from view till far into the day. The camp lay like a sunken island in a sea of fog and cold. The nights were uncannily quiet. The fog swallowed up the footsteps of the sentries and the crackling of the camp-fires.

In one such misty night Scipio and his legions escaped over the Trebia. Not even the Carthaginian outposts noticed that the Romans were withdrawing. When late the next morning the fog lifted and the alarm was sounded, the Numidians, Baleares, and Celts fell greedily upon the deserted camp for what booty they might find, instead of pursuing the enemy. Maharbal's horse troops only captured a few stragglers. The main forces of the Romans were already behind entrenchments in another camp. The Romans were masters in entrenchment. In a few hours they could stamp a camp out of the ground that would present an aggressor with complicated obstacles.

Carthalo was not satisfied till he heard that the new camp was only a few furlongs the other side of the Trebia. This seemed to suggest that Scipio was not planning flight but only evasion. 'Fear has got into his bones,' was Carthalo's verdict; 'he wants to have at least a river between himself and us.'

When towards evening Silenos came to find out how Carthalo was, he found him in better spirits than usual.

'You're like the elephants,' Silenos observed; 'you just can't stand the smell of the Romans. As soon as they're a little farther away you're better.'

'If only they don't escape us!'

'Where to?' Silenos wondered.

'Their country is a large one,' said Carthalo, and his face grew rapidly gloomy, 'and they have ships, they have the sea.' He was talking himself into a passion again. 'And all stolen from us,' he declared. 'Or do you tell me that they didn't build their ships on the model of ours? Overnight they had a fleet and they threw bridges from their ships on to ours, and by means of these devilish bridges they turned the ships into a piece of land on which they could fight as they were accustomed to fight. That

157

was their great fraud; that was how they took the sea from us. Am I not right?' Carthalo looked at Silenos with feverish eyes and went on without waiting for an answer. 'But this time we're not coming in ships, we're coming overland. And so what use are their ships and their devil's bridges to them? What use is our sea to them if we have their land?' Carthalo laughed, as if he had just put Rome—and Sicily—into his pocket. 'Let us tell tales about the Romans!' he suggested, turning his head towards me. 'He must know what they are really like. Let him get to know their heroes. Tell him the story of their Consul who was called Regulus! No,' he went on in the same breath, 'he shall first hear it from me as the Romans themselves tell it. Do you hear? Romans! Don't miss a word. In the first war that Rome waged on Carthage the Romans crossed the sea to Africa in order to conquer Carthage. Unfortunately the Consul in supreme command, who as a brave man fought in the front rank, fell into the hands of the Carthaginians. The Carthaginians wished to end the war as quickly as possible and they made a suggestion to the captured Consul, who was called Regulus. "You have forfeited your life," they said to him, "but we would rather you returned to Rome. The war is devouring you and us," they said; "make that clear to your people! If you are unsuccessful, give us your word of honour that you will return to us as a prisoner." So spoke the Carthaginians. And Regulus? He gave his word of honour and sailed back to Rome. And there? Listen carefully! He who held freedom in one hand, imprisonment and torture in the other, threw freedom away because it was mixed with shame, called on the Romans to continue the war until Carthage was a rubbish-heap. The noble man, true to his word, went back into the hands of his enemies, and the Carthaginians, beside themselves with rage at the failure of their plan, tore him to pieces like mad dogs. Now you tell the story,' he said to Silenos.

'Regulus,' said Silenos in a matter-of-fact tone, 'wanted to conquer Carthage. He set about it so clumsily that he was taken prisoner. To make bad matters worse he died in captivity. The Carthaginians announced his death to the Romans. When the

158

widow of the Consul heard the news she fell into immoderate grief and ordered two noble Carthaginians, Bostar and Hamilcar, whom she kept in her house as slaves, to be put to the torture, till Bostar fell dead and Hamilcar was crippled for life. In order to save the reputation of the Regulus family they published the story of the word of honour, the hero's return, and the monstrous slaughter of Regulus by the Carthaginians.'

'That's what they're like,' said Carthalo, 'capable of any kind of cruelty and falsehood.' He looked at me with burning eyes. 'Bostar dead, Hamilcar a cripple for life—think of that when we come to the day of reckoning with them.'

Carthalo suffered from the fact that day after day went by without the war making progress, as he said. At that time no one knew besides Hannibal and his closest advisers that a second Roman army was approaching. The Consul Sempronius was advancing in forced marches with the legions which had covered the southern part of the country until an attack by the Carthaginian fleet had come to nothing. Sempronius was an impetuous man. He was burning to prove his worth as a general. As soon as he reached the Roman camp beyond the Trebia, he urged Scipio, who had still not recovered from his wound, to attack the Carthaginians and to drive them out of the country. Hannibal was perfectly aware of the change caused by the arrival of Sempronius in the Roman camp. He had done nothing to hinder the meeting of the two armies. And now he was making no arrangements to take his army across the Trebia.

'We will leave that to the Romans,' he announced to his officers. With them and the allied captains he was making a survey on horseback of the country this side of the Trebia: the field on to which he hoped to entice the enemy. It was bounded by a stream that flowed into the Trebia. The stream had dug a deep bed for itself, it had steep cliffs on either side and shrubs on its banks. In this ambush a few hundred horsemen could be hidden. Hannibal put Mago in charge of this post. The remaining troops were to take up their position in the Trebia, avoid the enemy's onslaught, and thus give the impression that they didn't feel strong enough to engage him. Only the wings were to set up a determined resistance from the beginning. Hannibal wanted to entice the Romans into a trap and then to hem them in on three sides and to cut off their retreat over the river. From one of the flanks the elephants were to charge the cohorts and create confusion in their ranks.

Carthalo explained everything to me. There was no doubt in his mind that for the Romans the last day was at hand. He assured me that the elephants would turn the scale in this battle. He reminded me of all the orders and aids, and when I asked him whether he wouldn't be sitting on Suru with me his face grew grave. 'We are all targets and any one of us may be hit,' he explained, 'and I have the feeling that it will be me rather than you.'

I looked at him uncomfortably.

'Suru too may be hit.'

I was going to say something but he went on: 'When an elephant is hit he doesn't die immediately. Even severe wounds don't put him at once out of action. It is possible for him to go mad and then he is uncontrollable and may begin to trample down his own ranks. I have known that happen.'

'And what then?' I asked in alarm.

'Then the only thing is the chisel.'

I looked at him without understanding. Then he showed me a bag with a long sharp chisel in it and a heavy hammer. 'If you find the right spot for the chisel one good blow is enough and the raving is over. So is all his suffering.'

I stared at Carthalo.

'I don't suppose it will come to that,' he said to reassure me, 'and if it must be, then let us hope that I can do it for Suru. But you must know the spot in case I am hit first. I will mark it with a bit of colour so that you don't miss it if you have to do it. In war one must be prepared for everything.'

'Kill Suru?' I looked at Carthalo as if he was my enemy. The scar on his face began to throb.

'You mustn't misunderstand me,' said Carthalo excitedly.

'You need only do it if he begins to kill Carthaginians.' He
buckled the bag tightly on to the saddle, and after the elephants
had been fed he marked the mortal spot with a little red hook
that looked like the head of an arrow.

27

THE next day, from early morning onwards, Hannibal kept
Numidian horsemen riding round the Roman camp. They galloped up to the sentries and shot arrows at them. In the breasts of
the Consuls this skirmishing aroused increasing suspicion. At any
hour now they would have to expect Hannibal and his army to
cross the Trebia. As they themselves wanted a decisive action
they moved the legions out of the camp. Sempronius had persuaded Scipio that a further avoidance of the Carthaginians
would make them seem to be victors; only a battle would now
show who was master in the land.

On their return the Numidian horsemen reported that the
legions had been drawn up outside the Roman camp. They had
seen archers in coats of mail and helmets with chin-pieces,
swordsmen with curved shields, endless ranks of horsemen, and
now the rumour spread in the Carthaginian camp that the army
beyond the Trebia was superior in strength to their own. Even
among the officers there were anxious faces. Hannibal collected
the officers round him. 'Why, if the Romans are so strong, have
they hidden themselves away in their camp up till now?' he
asked sarcastically. 'It is possible that they are superior to us in
numbers—but that tells us nothing. The more live Romans there
are today over there, the more dead ones there will be here tomorrow. And do you suppose they have a Maharbal over there,
or a Monomach, or a Mago? And have they a Suru?'

After these questions Hannibal gave the officers their battle
orders. Numidian horsemen were to harass the Romans the
whole night long and deprive them of sleep. When morning
162

came more horsemen were to cross over and make feint attacks, evade the Roman counter-thrust, and lure them over the Trebia. 'They shall have a morning bathe, not we. They will arrive armoured in ice and it will hinder their fighting and split when we hit them. What more do you want?'

When the officers went back to their mercenaries their hesitation had vanished. They no longer had doubts about the result of the battle. Their confidence was communicated to their men. Everyone was certain that there was no escape for the Romans.

In the night it began to rain. The Romans were exposed to the cold showers on the open field. They spent the night in full armour because Numidian horsemen were continually harassing their outposts. Hannibal's mercenaries lay in their tents. Two hours before dawn Hannibal ordered them to be roused and fires to be lighted so that they could warm themselves. He also ordered a distribution of oil. We all rubbed ourselves well with it and thus had a second skin to protect us against the wet and the frost. It grew colder as the day broke. We were all given hot drinks and plenty to eat.

The day broke. It was the shortest day of the year. Rested and well-equipped, Hannibal's troops moved into their positions by the Trebia. Mago and his horse occupied the banks of the stream where he was to lie in ambush. The elephants, well-fed and in battle array, were drawn up round Suru. They were not holding a palaver. They were standing in a petrified silence, as if they knew what lay before them.

The Trebia gurgled uncannily. Usually a shallow river, it was swollen by the rain, and the cold muddy water rose up to the horses' flanks and the men's chests.

Very slowly it grew lighter. The elephants were drawn up in single file behind a little plateau. We could just see over the plateau and across the Trebia on to the large field over which the Romans would advance. We heard the cries of the Numidian horsemen as they attacked and withdrew alternately. Their cries grew louder, announcing that they were approaching the

163

Trebia. The Roman horse were forcing them back and putting them to flight.

'They're coming,' I heard Carthalo say behind me.

Behind our horsemen who were driving their horses through the river I saw their pursuers. They turned round at the Trebia. But now the Roman troops advanced on a wide front. The front ranks entered the river. The water came up to their chests. A hail of spears and arrows descended on them. Then our slingers and archers retired, and the Romans waded through the icy waters of the Trebia, holding their weapons above their heads.

'They are falling into the trap,' Carthalo panted, trembling with excitement. 'Now we've got them.'

The Romans began to force their way through our ranks. Their horse in wedge formation thrust forward. Men and animals became entangled. After that it was impossible to see anything clearly. The rain turned into snow. The sound of roars announced that the grim determination was growing on both sides. The Romans were still moving forward.

'Now Mago will engage them and then it will be our turn.' Carthalo took hold of my shoulders and shook them. I felt a choking sensation in my throat. Between my knees, fastened to the saddle, was the bag in which the chisel and hammer lay ready for use. A hand's breadth away from it, immediately behind the steep curve of the elephant's head, I could see the red mark between his ears. It looked as if an arrow had shot Suru there. It looked like blood—I could see nothing but this blood-red sign. The noise of battle increased; it beat over the hill like the roar of mighty breakers. Now the order came for the elephants to attack. A lane opened up in front of each of the grey giants. The elephants, already angered by the growing noise, entered these lanes growling. A sign was given and they began to run. And then they plunged into the midst of the battle.

'Vengeance for Hamilcar and Bostar!' Carthalo yelled behind me. I was afraid, not for myself, not for Carthalo—I was afraid for Suru.

164

Carthalo shouted orders. I knew by the sound of his voice that Suru was carrying them out obediently. He trampled down the legionaries towards whom Carthalo was driving him. I was staring down at Suru's body to see whether there was any blood on it.

'Trample down the murderers and the torturers!' Carthalo yelled.

Suru spread so much terror around him that everyone fled wherever he appeared. I only saw backs and helmets. No one had the courage to raise his weapon against Suru. But I was still afraid. I heard an elephant bellowing and soon others began to roar. Then Suru raised his trunk. He let out such a terrible noise that I grew stiff with fear. I had never before heard him roar like that, and now he became frantic as if he was ringed in by wild beasts. He turned first to one side, then to another, and finally he turned round and attacked the Carthaginians who had followed him.

'Is he wounded?' Carthalo yelled.

I could see no blood on Suru. Carthalo gave his orders desperately. He drove the iron hook into the space behind his ear. Suru grew only more and more beside himself. With his ears turned up he began to plunge and then he charged a way for himself through the Carthaginian troops who were to cut off the Romans' retreat.

'Give him the chisel!' Carthalo panted. 'He's out of his mind.' I seized the bag, snatched out the chisel and hammer, and pressed them tightly to myself.

'Give them to me!' Carthalo demanded threateningly. 'He's killing too many of our men.' Carthalo seized the hammer from me. And then I flung the chisel away into the driving snow. Carthalo began to roar like an animal. He forced me down and leaning over me began to strike at Suru's head with the hammer. The bunch of red feathers fell forward and the wind carried it away. Then Carthalo dropped the hammer. He released me and buried his face in his arms so as not to be able to see any more. Suru ran on through the ranks of the Carthaginians. He ran

165

until there was nothing to stop him, and even then he went on running. The noise of the battle died down behind us. Carthalo did nothing to bring Suru to a halt, and Suru dropped into a walking pace of his own accord. He walked quickly until he came to water. It was the stream by which Mago and his horsemen had hidden themselves, but here, some distance away from the Trebia, the banks were not steep. Suru stood still. Carthalo and I unstrapped ourselves from the saddle and dismounted. We took Suru's covering and armour off so that he could go down to the water. He submitted to everything. He waded into the water and began to wash himself. He washed himself as if he were covered all over with dirt.

Carthalo looked at him with empty eyes. His face was as grey as ashes. 'You've trampled Carthaginians to death,' he said in a hoarse voice. 'It's not as if you were wounded. Why did you do it?' Suru went on washing himself. He was washing away the horror that had taken possession of him. Even now that he had escaped from the battle he was so distraught that I began to doubt whether he was really Suru.

'He has killed Carthaginians. He has attacked Hannibal from behind,' Carthalo began again.

'He didn't know what he was doing,' I said.

'He did it. He didn't hold out to the end.'

'He just wanted to get out of it,' I said, trying to defend Suru.

'He ran away.' Carthalo spoke as if pronouncing judgement.

Suru lay down in the icy water; only his trunk was raised above it. Then he climbed on to the bank. Like a black impregnable rock he stood there in the snow. It was Suru again, the elephant I knew. I was tempted to run to him, but I was afraid of Carthalo's anger. All the time I was thinking: He has come through, he is alive, he isn't even wounded—and Carthalo wanted to kill him. Why? Why? I couldn't understand it.

'Why did you do it?' Carthalo turned suddenly on me. His face was angry. I didn't answer; I was afraid of him.

167

'He was cowardly,' Carthalo panted. 'I ought to have killed him as soon as he began to kill Carthaginians. He'll be no good for war any more. He'll always run away.'

It seemed as if Carthalo would never stop reproaching himself and me and Suru. He kicked at the spiked breast-plate as it lay on the ground. At that moment Suru started. We also sprang up. We heard a noise behind us. An isolated troop of Romans—at least a hundred of them—emerged from the driving snow and rushed towards us. They were all armed. I was rooted to the ground. So was Carthalo. But now Suru pushed past us. He began to growl. He raised his trunk, roared, and then charged at the troop of Romans, making the earth tremble beneath us. In their terror they threw their weapons away; we watched them running until they disappeared in the driving snow. Suru came back and posted himself beside his covering and his armour; he was still growling.

Carthalo collected himself. 'Now I must wash myself,' he said ruefully. '*I* was afraid.' He went down to the water but it was too cold for him. Then we set to work to collect the discarded weapons: lances and short two-edged swords. There was blood on the weapons. We made them into bundles and loaded them on to Suru. There were five heavy bundles. Carthalo left it to Suru to find the way back to the camp. Two hours later we arrived. Suru was treated as a hero. Carthalo turned a deaf ear to all the praise. But he made a pile of the captured weapons so that everyone could see them.

More and more troops of mercenaries appeared in the camp. The battle was decided. It was reported that half of the Romans who had crossed the Trebia were dead on the snowy field. The rest had found safety in flight.

No one went in pursuit of them. The deadly battle had exhausted the strength of the Carthaginians. Many of them too had fallen; there were gaps in every troop, and about half of the allies had disappeared in the snowstorm.

Towards evening the elephants who had survived collected round Suru. There were six. The rest lay dead on the battlefield,

168

ten grey mounds surrounded by dead men. The six survivors were wounded. All had lost blood, and they none of them lived through the cruel cold of the following night.

Suru was the only one who didn't die of cold. On the morning after the victory Hannibal had only one elephant left.

28

THE winter edged the Trebia with ice and buried the camp under snow. Unbroken frost made the ground hard as iron. It looked as if it would always be winter. For many weeks the snow and the ice edges didn't melt—but the army melted away. Many of the allies asked for leave of absence or disappeared without troubling about a pretext. In Carthalo's eyes they were 'mud, washed away by the rain', and the Romans were 'dirt that oozes through the fingers when one takes hold of it'. He quarrelled with the war—'a foul war'. He couldn't accept the idea that Hannibal won battle after battle and yet postponed the march on Rome. But above all Carthalo couldn't stop reproaching Suru and me and himself—'he and I and you have failed'—although Suru, as the only elephant who had come through, was admired even by the Carthaginian troops who had suffered losses through him. The mercenaries saw in him a guarantee that they too would outlast the war. They had all wrangled over the weapons that he had brought back as a prize. He had come without wounds out of a battle which had destroyed all the other elephants, and now the mercenaries considered him invulnerable and spoilt him so extravagantly that Carthalo had to put his foot down.

Since the battle Carthalo had been suffering from a deep-seated wound. He saw it as his fault that the Romans had been able to escape 'over the accursed mountains, the accursed rivers, and the accursed swamps', and neither Silenos, nor his friends among the Indos, could cure him of the idea. One day Synhal

169

said to him, 'You must get over this, just as Suru got over it. Only you can help yourself.'

But Carthalo turned a deaf ear to this and other like arguments. On the other hand he began to pick up greedily any piece of news about the war.

Sempronius, the Consul who had brought about the battle, had escaped and reached Rome. There the arrival of the beaten general had caused dismay, so the spies reported. Two new Consuls were elected and sent with new legions to the winter camps in which the remnants of the beaten army had taken refuge. Hannibal ordered these camps to be harassed continuously. In spite of the bitter cold Hannibal didn't stay in the camp, but tried to seize some of the settlements in the neighbourhood in order to come at stocks of food. While attacking a trading settlement on the Po which was protected by a strong fort he was wounded. He allowed himself and his horsemen five days' rest. Then he advanced against the Roman town Victumulae. The garrison felt strong enough to go out to meet him. Hannibal beat them and entered the town together with the fugitives. The order went out to the defenders of the town to surrender their weapons. After that had been done Hannibal handed over the town to his mercenaries for plunder. The booty which they brought back to the camp raised the spirits of the whole army.

Wherever the Romans tried to engage Hannibal they were beaten or put to flight. But bad news was coming from Iberia, from the new Carthage. One of the Scipios had landed there and had by cunning moves won over a number of Iberian tribes. He had even been able to form new cohorts out of auxiliary troops. In a clash with the Carthaginians by the Ebro he beat them so thoroughly that their losses were six thousand dead and still more prisoners. Their camp fell into the hands of the victors. The Romans seized some of the coastal towns and soon had a large part of the country in their power. The new Carthage, which Hannibal had entrusted to his brother Hasdrubal, was crumbling away under the feet of Roman cohorts. But Hannibal would not think of turning back.

As soon as the sun began to lick the snow away Hannibal ordered his men to break camp. He trusted that the sun would also uncover the roads in the mountains and make it possible for a whole army to use them. Hannibal wanted to march over the Apennines into Etruria, get the Etruscans on to his side by friendly means or by threats, open up their rich towns for his mercenaries and take the interior of the country from the Romans.

The warm weather lasted a few days. The army climbed to the top of the Apennines. Hannibal was riding on Suru. He was in a cheerful mood and infected everyone round him with it, even Carthalo. The ice seemed to have broken up for the year.

Then suddenly, just after we had reached the crest of the mountains, the weather changed with a violence that took our breath away. A snowstorm that made any further advance impossible fell upon us. We took what shelter there was to be found in hollows, and built up rough walls with heavy stones, behind which we crouched. It was impossible to set up tents.

On the second day Suru's eyes were stuck together. He was distraught by the wind and wouldn't eat anything. The snowstorm tore at the army and penned it up in little groups together. It was colder than it had been on the pass in the Alps. The wind swept over us with rain in the day-time, with snow during the nights, and kept us pressed down on to the hard frozen earth. We were besieged, and a sally was out of the question. For what seemed an endless period of time we were held down by a force against which weapons were powerless. Carthalo and I had settled down as well as we could by Suru. Carthalo had a fever; he could no longer stand upright. Silenos and Synhal appeared now and again and brought us food. When the third night came Carthalo sent me to Silenos. He was quieter than usual. The wind too was dying down. Silenos came back with me at once. He tried to build up a hearth and managed to light a fire. Carthalo looked at the glow with shining eyes. He wouldn't eat anything but drank greedily when Silenos offered him drink. He drank up half a skin of water.

M   171

'It's the last time I shall drink,' he said in apology.

'You ought to sleep now,' Silenos told him.

'Soon I shall have my fill of sleep,' Carthalo protested. 'But first I want to talk to you two. It's all over for me. Even this accursed wind has noticed it and has died down a little so that I can talk to you. Look at Suru! In spite of his gummed eyelids he's seen how it is with me.'

Suru was standing half turned away and his great head was low. His trunk and lower lip hung slackly down. All over his body his skin was hanging in folds. He looked very old, as if he had lived through many years in the past few days. His life seemed to be concentrated in his ears which were raised a little.

'He's listening to me,' Carthalo told us, 'but I've said all I have to say to him. I'm not angry with him any more for losing his head. Everyone is afraid once in a lifetime. Now he's got over it and so have I.' Carthalo looked at me. 'Don't desert him! He's attached to you. He found you buried in the rubble and saw to it that we got you out. You owe it to him to stay with him. And you,' he said to Silenos, 'take care of the boy, as I have taken care of him. Let him become a Carthalo.' He looked at the fire. It was getting difficult for him to speak. 'You're neither of you Carthaginians as I am, but both of you—like me—are devoted to Hannibal. Nothing else matters.' He raised his eyes to look at Silenos. 'How good that you made a fire!'

'It's lucky that the wind has dropped,' said Silenos, 'or it would have put the fire out. Go to sleep now!'

But Carthalo wouldn't listen to him. 'You will get to Carthage,' he said, and now there was more life in his voice. 'You will climb the steep streets where they make braziers and lamps with beaks, panniers for the water-bottles, pots, baskets, and wall-hangings and cedarwood chests. You will smell the wood and the bakeries; you will hear the hammers with which the smiths beat the copper. You will see the town that sparkles like no other town under the sun. Suru will lead you to his stable in the wall,' Carthalo whispered to me. 'Oh, nothing will seem strange to you, not even the gods! They are stern gods,' he said,

172

'but they have made Carthage what it is. They know no mercy. Anath is full of fury; he mows the enemy down with his sickle and heads lie as thickly about him as swarms of locusts. With his sickle he cuts his brother Moth into pieces and throws them over the fields as a farmer sows his seed. Hadad riding on his horse tramples all his enemies underfoot. Baal turns into Moloch and devours all the children that are brought to him. We cannot do without sacrifices. Whenever we have tried to placate Moloch with cripples or slave children he has avenged himself and brought Carthage to the brink of destruction. The gods of Carthage demand our firstborn. The first man who in primeval times made a boat out of a tree and sailed out to sea in it, sacrificed his boat to the gods on the island which he reached. Dido, who built Carthage, burned herself to death when an African king wanted to bind her to himself. Carthaginian tin traders, pursued by pirates, drove their sailing ships on to the rocks in order not to betray to strangers the way to the land of tin. Sacrifices have made Carthage great. Never has a Carthaginian considered himself more important than Carthage.' Carthalo seized our hands. 'The old Carthalo marched over the Alps for the sake of Carthage; he marched as far as his legs would carry him—the young Carthalo will go on from where the old one stopped and will take care of Suru and see that he comes safely home to Carthage. We can never be destroyed so long as we think like this. I am going to die now,' he said breathing with difficulty, 'but Carthage will live. And Rome will be destroyed. Hannibal will punish Rome for trying to enslave Carthage. He will do to the Romans what they did to Hamilcar and Bostar—and to me. Take my dagger,' he said, 'and cut the strap.'

He held his right wrist out to me. I pushed the blade under the strap and cut it through. We saw a brand on the white skin.

'I have always kept it hidden,' said Carthalo, his breath coming in gasps. 'But you shall see it now and hear the whole story. As a young man in the first war I fell into their hands. My elephant was dead and I myself was wounded. They branded me

174

with this mark as though I had been one of their cattle. They also put me to the torture. They wanted to get out of me all I could tell them of our elephant lore. When I couldn't bear the pain any longer I began to talk. But I lied to them; every word I said was untrue. They stopped flaying me because I had told them so much. Two years later I escaped. When I reached the coast I took a boat. In those days the sea still belonged to Carthage and I met a Carthaginian ship—I was free!' Carthalo struggled for breath. 'Keep the dagger,' he gasped; 'strike down the first Roman you meet with it. Carthalo is dying, but his hatred must not die with him. You are Carthalo now, you will hate them——' Those were his last words. Carthalo looked at me so fixedly that I felt afraid. The reflection of the fire made his face look fiercely alive. But he was dead.

Suru had raised his head. He took one or two uncertain steps. Then he raised his trunk. It looked as if he were going to bellow. But his trunk dropped again; he groaned and then stood lost in contemplation as before.

29

THE calm weather lasted and on the next day the army set out again. Hannibal turned round; he no longer trusted the spring. He would postpone the crossing of the mountains till he could be certain of the weather. Rejected by the Apennines, he marched down on to the plain where winter had held us prisoner.

Where we were going to was all one and the same to me. Silenos looked after me. And Suru was there, and Hannibal rode on him sitting behind me. These three were left to me: Silenos, Suru, and Hannibal.

Hannibal didn't always ride on Suru. He often rode one of his horses, and sometimes he went on foot like the mercenaries. He underwent all the hardships that they had to endure. He slept in the midst of them, on the bare ground as they did, covered with his cloak which was now crusted over with mud—its redness had disappeared.

Hannibal marched nearly up to Placentia. Thrown back on to the positions which he had occupied several months ago, Hannibal was waiting for a sun strong enough to harden the subsoil and make the roads safe. The rivers, still swollen by the downpours of rain and the melting snows, had overflowed their banks and kept the plain under water.

'How long will it go on like this?' I asked Silenos.

'Do you mean the floods?'

'I mean the war.'

Silenos looked at me without saying anything.

'Months?'

'Years,' said Silenos.

'Three? Five?'

'Perhaps ten. Or twenty.'

I looked across the grey expanse of water, at the roads with no surface which led down to the plain. I thought of our allies who had come quickly and disappeared again quickly.

'What does Hannibal say?' I dared to ask.

'He is used to war,' Silenos replied. 'He wouldn't think of giving up. And he will be able to get everyone in his army to agree with him. His mercenaries are hungry, they are wounded and look like beggars, but he makes them feel they are the masters of the world. All these weeks we've been held up, have you seen any sign of mutiny? There never will be any, because Hannibal is the kind of man all his mercenaries would like to be: hard, brave, never to be beaten. He has lost his most important weapon: the elephants—except for one. He marches on. And the mercenaries follow him. He is the only god they believe in. He knows that Rome lies behind the Romans, and that Carthage is far away—that doesn't upset him. He puts his trust in himself and in those who march with him.'

I couldn't take my eyes off Silenos' face. 'And why are you marching with him? You were against the war.'

'I am against war,' said Silenos. 'But now there is a war and I

176

want to be in it. How could I ever write down what everything was like if I hadn't taken part in it myself?'

My thoughts went to Suru, and I was suddenly afraid of the next battle.

'Will Hannibal use just this one elephant?' I asked Silenos.

'He will try to get him safely through,' Silenos said. 'You know how fond he is of him.'

Since the death of Carthalo, Suru and I were kept nearer Hannibal than ever. Sometimes he rode about the surrounding country on Suru in order to test the firmness of the roads. Much of the land was still buried under mud.

Suru's eyes were healthy again. But Hannibal's left eye in which inflammation had set up in the mountains would not heal in spite of all the attention given to it. Hannibal didn't spare himself or allow himself much sleep. From afar you could recognize him by the bandage which covered his forehead and half his left cheek. I never heard him complain, although, as I heard from Synhal, he was always in pain.

I kept his clothes and his weapons in order and was often in his tent. When the bad eye was more than usually painful he lay stretched out on his bed. At those times he didn't talk and kept his good eye shut. I heard by his breathing whether he was awake or asleep. Mostly he was awake.

Once when he was lying like that, awake but with his eyes shut, I noticed that something was sticking out of his broad belt which was hanging on one of the tent-poles. It was a phial of blue glass, unusually small and flatter than my little finger. Just as I was going to push it back into the belt Hannibal started up. He asked me for the belt, pushed the phial back himself into the hidden pocket, and carefully fastened the little buckle which had come undone. He looked at me for a long time out of his one eye. 'It's only a last resort,' he said. 'They shan't capture me alive.'

He gave me the belt. 'You haven't seen anything.'

'I don't know anything about it,' I said, feeling rather frightened.

He lay back again. 'Now we have two secrets,' he said, and his voice was calm again, 'the dream about the dragon, and the phial in the belt. Even Silenos doesn't know about that.' He was silent for a time and then began to talk about Suru. 'You get on well with him,' he said, 'better than Carthalo did.'

'Carthalo was a good driver,' I said.

'He was,' Hannibal agreed, 'but you are my little Carthaginian.'

I kept on thinking of the blue phial. When I had left the tent the question began to gnaw at me: why does he carry poison about with him? Is he reckoning on the possibility of failure? Does he want to leave a back door open—a way out when there is no way on? Is he afraid of an end that won't lie in his hands? These thoughts worried me, and once or twice I nearly gave in to the temptation to share my secret with Silenos. But I didn't, even when he came upon me one day brooding over what the phial meant.

One day Hannibal appeared without the bandage. He had torn it off. His left eye was dead. Under the left half of his forehead there was a dark slit.

'A one-eyed man on a one-tusked animal,' he said mockingly, when at last the procession began to move again. The army crossed the mountains without much difficulty this time. But then came the marshes. The mercenaries often had to march with the water up to their knees. Mercenaries and horses were lost in the mists. Only Suru towered above them, like a grey hill, moving like a phantom. Hannibal sat in silence behind me on the saddle which was padded with cushions of goat's hair.

Many fell sick in the marshes. Hannibal didn't pay them any attention. He was doing what he could for the healthy ones. He sent horsemen into the settlements that lay beside our road with orders to take whatever was to be taken. Anyone who resisted lost not only all his possessions.

'I won't let hunger rob me of a single man,' said Hannibal.

After four days and three nights the marshes came to an end. A few furlongs from Lake Trasimenus Hannibal ordered the army to encamp. Two days later it was reported to him that the Roman legions were advancing towards us from the north.

'Now we'll get to grips with them,' said Hannibal to his intimate advisers, 'and not far from here.'

During the last two days he had inspected the country round our camp, and had discovered the most favourable place to set a trap. When night fell he ordered camp-fires to be lighted and left a rear-guard behind to tend them. The Romans were now within sight. As soon as it was completely dark Hannibal moved his army away towards the south along the foot of the Cortonian Mountains.

Hannibal knew that the Consul Flaminius, now general of the Roman army, was a dare-devil like Sempronius. He had started off in such a hurry to put the Carthaginian army to flight that his horse had bucked and thrown him off head over heels. When this was reported to Hannibal he said: 'The horse knew the fate that is in store for his rider.'

While Hannibal was showing his troops their positions he rode one of his horses. But towards morning he mounted Suru. By his face I knew that everything was driving towards a decisive battle.

30

THE Cortonian Mountains come down so close to the edge or Lake Trasimenus that there is only a narrow passage-way from the north to the south. On the road that runs along the shore of the lake there is room for an army to match but not to be drawn up in battle order. A broad belt of reeds, rooted in marshy soil, surrounds the lake. Farther out it becomes deeper. The Cortonian Mountains do not rise up steeply, but if the heights are occupied an escape over them is as good as impossible.

Hannibal linked height to height with chains of slingers and other lightly armed troops. He posted his most tried and trusty

179

mercenaries and horse troops in the ravines. Numidians on fast horses were holding themselves in readiness to bar the defile at both ends. By the time that day dawned the trap was set for the Romans. The lake made its contribution: it covered the strip of shore with thick fog and turned the ravines into pools of mist. Only the heights were clear.

At sunrise the mist began to gleam with a blood-red light. Hannibal, sitting behind me on Suru, looked down at the trap with a satisfied air.

'No one will escape out of it,' he said. A dark fire was glowing in his eye. 'The mist is taking half our work away from us.'

I asked whether Suru would be in the battle.

'Are you afraid for him?' Hannibal tapped me on the shoulder comfortingly. 'He won't come to any harm—you've seen that for yourself. No one can touch him.'

It was quiet by the lake and on the mountain-tops. Everything depended on the enemy falling into the trap without his suspicion being aroused. No tell-tale sounds must come from the ambush which stretched along the lakeside. The mercenaries and horsemen knew this and lay on the watch without so much as whispering to one another.

Larks rose up out of the mist and hung lost in the blue, but they soon fell down again into their great white nest.

Then came the clatter of horses' hoofs. The Carthaginian rear-guard, who had been in charge of the camp-fires, withdrew hastily into the narrow defile. Their orders were to keep in contact with the enemy without engaging them in battle. Only farther south, on the open ground where Maharbal was waiting with his horse troops, were they to bring the enemy to a stand and cut off their escape out of the defile.

The clatter grew louder. Roman horse troops were on the heels of the rear-guard. Now they were joined by foot soldiers. It was a march of noisy phantoms as the Romans tried to find their way under the blanket of mist.

'It couldn't be better,' said Hannibal to Mago and Monomach and the other officers who had collected round him to receive their orders for the attack and to carry them back to their troops.

One of the officers from the rear-guard emerged from the mist and came riding up the hill as fast as his horse would carry him. He reported that the Romans had broken into the camp at early dawn. Astonished at finding it deserted, they had scattered the fires and then immediately set out in pursuit.

'Their ardour has not yet diminished,' Hannibal said mockingly, pointing down to the mist out of which the noise of marching legions rose. As the tramping of the vanguard revealed, their front ranks were already more than half-way through the defile. 'They can take their time,' remarked Hannibal. 'They have the longest day of the year before them—and so have we.' He sent the officers back to their troops, keeping a detachment of Berserkers and thirty horsemen with himself. The Berserkers were to clash their weapons together and roar as they alone could roar, when the time came to give the Carthaginians the signal to fall upon the Romans.

The mist was beginning to disperse. In some places the pools of mist lifted and helmets and armour caught the light. The Romans were advancing without any suspicion.

Now a horseman arrived from the north end of the defile. He reported that the last of the legionaries had moved in. Hannibal raised his arm. The Berserkers roared and made such a crashing noise with their weapons that Suru's ears rose up and he lifted his trunk in displeasure. I was able to quieten him, as the Berserkers were already charging down the hill and the mist was swallowing them up. Now the sound of battle was coming from all along the lake. In echelon formation the Carthaginians pressed down on to the Romans, who now realized with horror that they were encircled.

The mist was dispersing quickly. Hannibal on Suru's back was on the look-out as if from a tower. Now what was happening down by the lake took on clear outlines. Some of the Romans were defending themselves with grim determination, others were taking flight and dragging fighting cohorts along with them.

Many were trying to find a way of escape for themselves. But the ravines and the heights were barred to them. Only the lake was open to them. Some of the most desperate tried to hide in the belt of reeds and sank in the swamp. Several jumped into the lake and began to swim but their armour pulled them down. After two hours of battle there were none left but isolated fugitives, running or riding for their lives. At one spot only a cohort was left, fighting in regular battle formation. It was still defending itself when the mist had dispersed. Hannibal told me to ride towards it.

'The Consul is there, fighting for his life,' he said. 'He mustn't be allowed to escape.'

Suddenly Suru stood still and threw his trunk into the air and the horses of Hannibal's mounted escort tried to bolt.

'What was that?' Hannibal asked his horsemen.

'It was an earthquake!' some of them shouted back to him.

'The terror of the Romans has infected the earth,' said Hannibal mockingly.

'It was a real earthquake,' the horsemen maintained, and one of them pointed to the lake. Big waves were coming in although there was a complete calm.

'An earthquake, you're right,' said Hannibal in a voice that all could hear. 'Italy is trembling before us. Let us hope that it doesn't break into pieces.'

He ordered Suru and his escort to move on to the hill immediately above the fighting cohort. It was now completely surrounded. More and more Carthaginians were thrusting on to it. Along the lake there were countless rows of dead, chiefly Romans. There were still plenty of Carthaginians looking out for the enemy.

'It's going according to the plan,' I heard the man say who was sitting behind me on Suru. From these words, and still more from the silence that followed them, I felt the tremendous willpower with which he had set the avalanche of destruction in motion and with which he had directed mercenaries, horses and their riders so that there was no way out for the Romans but death. And if anyone had told me at that moment that Hannibal had put the lake and the mountains where they were now, that he had arranged the belt of reeds, the ravines, and defiles so that they would serve for an ambush, that he had ordered the mist to rise and the earth to quake—I would have believed it. The mist had lain there just as long as was necessary to keep the trap hidden; it had lifted to show the Romans that there was no escape for them. Everything had helped to make Hannibal's victory complete.

The one cohort that was still fighting was dwindling away. Finally a detachment of Berserkers, in wedge formation, fought their way into it and up to the Consul. Flaminius fell, mortally wounded by a spear. The survivors now tried to fight their way out.

'Strike them down!' Hannibal yelled.

Never before had I heard a human being yell like that. It was the cry of a beast of prey, about to spring for a kill.

Hannibal urged the horsemen to pursue a small group of Romans who had fought their way out. 'Don't let any escape!'

Then ten or twelve Romans appeared from the other side, as if Hannibal's terrible cry had drawn them to him. Their weapons were covered with blood. It was a lost troop, and they were not looking for a way of escape but rather for a desperate action. They rushed at Hannibal. The legionaries had recognized him. That man in the red cloak, riding on the only elephant there was in the whole country, could be no one but Hannibal. They were breathless with running and their faces were distorted with hatred.

'Come to your death!' Hannibal shouted. He pulled his short sword out of its scabbard. I held the shield so that it protected both him and me in front.

When Suru saw the Romans he growled angrily. As this didn't bring them to a halt he began to attack them. Hannibal shouted again and Suru fell into a frenzy. The Romans surrounded him. He trampled two of them down and dealt a deadly blow with his trunk to two others. He struck the spear

183

out of another's hand, seized him, and flung him into the air. He
roared, and now Carthaginians came to our help from all sides,
on foot and on horseback. The Romans who were still alive
flung their spears at Hannibal. He beat off spear after spear with
his sword. Now the Romans were surrounded, and they flung
their swords at Hannibal in the hope of hitting him. He laughed

184

and beat off sword after sword. He fought as one whom nothing can touch. He only missed one sword. It struck my right arm and tore it open from the shoulder to the elbow.

A few minutes later the Romans were all cut down. Until the last their eyes had been fixed on Hannibal and they had cursed him.

'They got you,' I heard Hannibal say. 'We'll soon have you bandaged up. Make Suru kneel down!'

Suru knelt down without waiting for the order from me.

'I've never had a better elephant,' said Hannibal, dismounting, 'and never a better driver.' He examined my wound. 'No one of your mettle would die of that,' he said.

Suru didn't stand up again, as he otherwise always did when he was rid of his load.

'He's killed five,' Hannibal cried to the officers and mercenaries. 'Let him be an example to you!'

'Stand up, Suru,' I said coaxingly, while my wound was being bandaged. He made an effort to get up but fell back on to his knees.

'Stand up!' I said again. 'It's all over.'

'Stand up, old fellow!' Hannibal now joined in. 'You've saved my life and the little Carthaginian's. The war will soon be over—stand up!'

And now with a great effort Suru did stand up. Then I saw streaks of blood on the grey pillars that supported him. On his neck and on his shoulder there were gaping wounds the size of the palm of my hand.

'What have you been doing, old fellow?' asked Hannibal in alarm.

I tore myself away from the man who was bandaging me and took a few steps towards Suru. Then I fell flat on my face and knew no more.

31

WHEN I came to myself I was lying in Hannibal's tent. Silenos was sitting by me.

'Where is Suru?' I asked.

'Don't worry about him,' said Silenos.

I tried to get up.

186

Hannibal came over to me. 'Lie still!' he said severely.'You must get well. I can't do without you.'

'How is Suru?' I asked him.

'He walked of his own accord behind you when we carried you away,' said Hannibal.

I looked at Silenos, and he confirmed this. 'Not even a driver was necessary. He walked behind you like a lamb.'

Hannibal went back to Mago and Monomach who were with him in the tent and he sat down again.

'Try to go to sleep now,' said Silenos softly.

I shut my eyes and saw Suru standing before me as I had last seen him. My wound was painful. The thoughts gnawed at me: Why did he yell like that? The battle was over, surely? Why did he yell? With that terrible yell he drew the battle down on to Suru, and now Suru is wounded.

Hannibal and Mago and Monomach were talking about the battle. They were talking loudly; I only caught scraps of their conversation: '. . . to the last man. . . . That will be the finishing stroke for Rome. . . .'

'A few thousand have escaped,' said Mago indignantly.

'The horse troops are to blame for that!' Monomach maintained.

Hannibal tried to calm him down. 'Maharbal is after them. They were foot soldiers. He must have caught them up long ago. He will soon be here to report that they don't exist any more.' Hannibal's voice sounded like Monomach's. They were all talking in a way that made it difficult to tell who was speaking. Sometimes they disagreed. My wound hurt me. Why did he yell? Now Suru is wounded. My head was resounding with that terrible cry. After a time none of their voices reached me—nor did any other sound. When I woke up again I heard a new voice. It was Maharbal's voice. There was no hatred in it and there were no reservations. I listened to it and could hear every word he said.

'After two hours we caught them up. They turned and faced us on a hill,' he reported. 'They made a fort out of the hill, without a single trench, with nothing but the courage with which they defended themselves. There were more of us than of them, and they knew that there was no longer an army that could rescue them. But they fought as if the victory depended on them. We lost more men than they did.'

'But in the end you finished them off?' Monomach asked impatiently.

'It would have been senseless to go on fighting,' said Maharbal calmly. 'I broke off the battle when I saw that it would cost the lives of a few more thousands of our men.'

'You just gave up?' asked Mago in an outraged voice.

'I made the Romans an offer,' said Maharbal.

'They fraternized,' said Monomach sarcastically.

Maharbal didn't let himself be disconcerted. 'I demanded their weapons, and in return I promised them safe withdrawal.'

'And they?'

'Laid down their weapons.'

'And you let them go?' Mago stood up in his excitement.

'I came here to ask for permission to do that,' Maharbal explained.

'You have, let us hope, surrounded them,' said Monomach spitefully.

'No,' answered Maharbal.

There was a deathlike stillness in the tent. I moved my head so that I could see Hannibal. All faces were turned towards him.

'How many?' he asked without looking at Maharbal.

'About six thousand,' Maharbal answered.

'All Romans?'

'No,' said Maharbal, 'there are some auxiliaries among them.'

Hannibal looked at him. 'You will sift out the Romans.'

'I don't understand,' said Maharbal.

Then Hannibal explained. 'We will let the non-Romans go, so that they give a good account of us at home. But we will make all the Romans into slaves—which is what they deserve.'

'I gave them my word,' said Maharbal, who could only just control his voice.

188

Hannibal held the palm of one hand up to his face and blew over it, as though he were puffing a feather across to Maharbal. 'Here it is back again.'

Maharbal turned pale. 'They didn't fight like Romans,' he said; 'their swords would have cut down a few more thousand of your men. They gave up their weapons because they trusted my word.'

'And will get themselves supplied with new weapons if we let them go,' Hannibal interrupted him. 'Do you suppose that they will then kill fewer of our men?'

Maharbal didn't answer.

'You don't understand that?' asked Hannibal sharply.

'No,' said Maharbal, beside himself with excitement. 'This isn't war any longer, it's murder.'

Then Hannibal stood up. Everyone got up. Hannibal walked up to Maharbal threateningly. 'You think you can teach me what is war and what is murder?' he asked in a trembling voice. 'You will prescribe what I may and what I may not do? You presumptuous man! Let me tell you once and for all: in war everything is allowed that does harm to the enemy. And whatever kills the enemy is good and we don't ask any questions about it. For the enemy there is only one feeling: hatred. War isn't a tournament, it's bitter earnest. Are the Romans to be slaves, or are we? Are they or we to be masters of the world? These are the issues. Do you want them to trample us underfoot, to treat you and me as they treated Bostar and Hamilcar? Listen to me, you friend of murderers! If Rome doesn't fall, then Carthage will. To save Carthage we have to do some hard things—it may be we have to break our word. Let me tell you this: those two councillors, who were thrown down from the walls of Saguntum because they sided with us, owe their deaths to me.'

'To you?' said Maharbal in horror.

'Because it was necessary,' said Hannibal coldly. 'The ball had to be set rolling; the Romans had to be put in the wrong in the eyes of the whole world. That object was achieved by what I did. Nobody could help thinking that the Romans had incited

189

the two councillors. For who—except me—would get the idea into his head that a Carthaginian had started the agitation against Carthage?' Hannibal gave Maharbal a contemptuous look. 'That is how war is waged,' he said. 'I hope you know now what you've got to do, you duffer! Or are you going to attack me in the rear?'

Maharbal had stepped back.

'What are you waiting for?' Hannibal shouted.

'I can't do it,' he said, and his voice had become a whisper.

Then the black slit which had now no eye in it opened, and a terrible look fell on Maharbal. 'You will sift them out!' Hannibal panted. 'You and no one else. I give you half the night to do it in. Go! And don't let my eyes'—*eyes* he said, although he had only one eye left—'fall on you again until you have carried out my orders. Orders are orders!'

To this there was no reply. Maharbal was so thunderstruck that he staggered as he walked away. He walked like a wounded man. Hannibal stared at him as he went. The look on his face was more than I could bear. It was as if he had just killed someone.

I pulled Silenos by the arm and sat up. 'Help me out of the tent,' I whispered to him.

Silenos helped me to stand up. I could walk by myself. Hannibal was still staring in front of him with a distorted face that reminded me of Monomach's. He didn't notice us going out. He said nothing, and the others too were silent. I began to be afraid of Hannibal.

'Where is Suru?' I asked Silenos as soon as we were outside the tent. It was already getting dark.

'Come,' said Silenos. He took me by the arm that wasn't wounded and led me to his tent.

'Where is Suru?' Fear rose up within me and made my throat feel tight. Silenos drew me into his tent. I asked him for the third time.

He looked at me; his face was twitching. Then I knew that Suru was dead.

190

32

SILENOS led me up to his bed. I took the few necessary steps automatically. I lay there without a word, staring at the tent ceiling. As soon as I shut my eyes I saw Suru, with gaping wounds on his neck and streaks of blood on his legs.

The tent door was open and cool air flowed in. The day was nearly over, the longest day of the year—so Hannibal had said when it broke. Then he had been sitting behind me on Suru. Now Suru was dead; night was coming and nothing would stop it.

Silenos lighted a lamp. He shut the door of the tent and then sat down by me. His face was as bright as if all the light in the tent had settled on it. I had never seen this face distorted.

'How is the arm?' he asked.

'It doesn't hurt any more,' I said, although it did hurt.

'You will feel better tomorrow,' Silenos assured me. 'You were lucky: it isn't a deep wound.' He put his hand on my forehead and counted the pulse-beats at my wrist. 'I'll give you something to drink to make you sleep well,' he said. 'It's the shortest night in the year—you must go to sleep quickly.'

He was getting up to fetch the medicine but I held him back. 'Is it true that he walked behind me?'

'He walked behind you, without a driver,' Silenos said again. 'He walked behind you till he couldn't walk any farther.'

I thought of the two wounds that I had seen on Suru. They hadn't been any bigger than the wound Carthalo had given him to heal him. 'There were only two wounds and they were no bigger than the palm of my hand,' I argued.

'You didn't see what was on the other side,' said Silenos.

I urged him to tell me everything. He looked at me searchingly.

And then he told me how it had all happened. They had walked round Suru and had discovered terrible wounds on him.

A sword was sticking in him up to the hilt. A lance had gone so deep that only half of it was to be seen. When Hannibal had pulled out the sword and the lance, Suru had let out a great cry of pain as if he had just been given a deadly wound. He had bel-

lowed in such a way that everyone, even Hannibal, turned stiff
with horror. 'It was as if he was lifting up his voice in mourning
for all the other elephants who had met death before him, all
those who had started out with him and were now dead. All
the while his four feet were standing in his own blood. Some of
the mercenaries had laid you on a blanket when your arm was
bandaged and now they were carrying you away. Then Suru

set himself in motion and walked behind you. He wanted to be near you. Even getting up on to his feet was an almost unbelievable achievement, considering the severity of his wounds, and now he walked behind you although every step must have been torture for him. He wanted to show that he belonged to you, and he walked behind you till his legs could no longer carry his enormous wounded body. He didn't want to be separated from you. When he broke down there wasn't even enough strength left in him for a cry. He groaned but it was a groan that you could hardly hear; his look told us how much he was suffering. Hannibal couldn't bear to watch this suffering any longer. He looked for the hammer and chisel, but the bag fastened to the elephant's saddle was empty. Then Hannibal drew his short sword and picked up a heavy stone. And then he did the deed, and he left his sword to the elephant whose sufferings were at last over. Now you know everything.'

'Why did he do it?' I asked bitterly.

'He wanted to help him. A few blows were enough.'

'He killed him before that; he killed him with that shout he gave.' I was accusing Hannibal. 'Why did he have to shout? That was what killed Suru.'

Silenos gave up trying to defend him. My wound was hurting me. The thought that Hannibal had killed Suru was gnawing at me. He had all the elephants on his conscience. Out of thirty-nine elephants thirty-nine were dead, just because he used them wrongfully for his war. Then I thought of Maharbal, and Hannibal's terrible words rang in my ears: 'It was I who caused the two councillors of Saguntum to be thrown from the city wall because they sided with us. . . .' And so it was he who destroyed Saguntum, not the Romans. Carthalo had lied to me, or else he didn't know the truth because Hannibal had lied to him—and to everyone else in his army. He had promised them victories—I saw before me unending ranks of dead men, the dead by the lake, the dead by the rivers, the dead in the ravines. I saw Barmokar and Myrkan standing at the whipping-posts, and I remembered, word for word, everything that Myrkan had shouted to Hannibal.

'Myrkan was right,' I said aloud. 'He will kill more men than his father Barca did.'

Silenos heard everything I said without a word of contradiction.

'I thought I would never leave him,' I went on, 'but now I'm going to.'

'Where will you go?' asked Silenos anxiously.

'I shall find some place where there's no war and stay there.'

'Let your wound heal first,' said Silenos; 'then things will arrange themselves.'

I looked at the face I knew so well, I looked into his eyes, and I saw that they were hiding nothing, and suddenly I realized that he was the only human being left that belonged to me.

'And you?' I asked. 'What will you do?'

'His war isn't my war,' said Silenos, 'but as long as this war lasts my place is at his side.'

I looked at him without understanding.

'If anyone can understand me, then you can, you alone among all those who are marching with him,' said Silenos. 'They are all mercenaries—except you and me. All of them allowed themselves to be bought by him; they've all made his war into their war and have given up what they once were for what he has wanted them to be—even Maharbal. They let him do their thinking for them, and they do what he asks of them. I couldn't do what Maharbal did but then I'm not fighting for Carthage. What have I got to fight with?—I haven't even got a dagger. And if Hannibal ever ordered me to kill a man I wouldn't do it.'

'It would cost you your life,' I said.

'That is possible,' said Silenos. 'But as long as he lets me go my own way I will stay with him. I must find out what sort of man he really is, and only someone who keeps him always in view can do that. You know him better than most of them know him—but did you know yesterday that he could kill a man with a look? As it happened you were there today when he did, and so was I. I am more with him than anyone else. He confides in me more than in his brothers, and he doesn't know that by

195

confiding in me he is doing me a service. That is my adventure: to read in his face the book I am going to write. That keeps me with him. I have nothing to do with his people. I am afraid of the gods of Carthage, and as the gods of a country are, so are the people. I have been in Carthage; I have seen for myself what the Carthaginians are like. They crucify not only their generals who lose battles—but also lions! Yes, at the edge of the desert I have seen crosses with lions nailed to them, all because these lions had strayed into their herds. I love lions—how can I love Carthage? But I will stand by Hannibal till the end. In him I can take hold of war by its roots. When he calls me to him he talks—nothing will stop him talking. He has never asked for my advice. He feels himself high above everyone and despises even those nearest to him. You saw how he treated Maharbal. He is a man who has taken the oath at Moloch's altar. Later generations must see what such a man is like—perhaps then, when another man of his kind appears among them, they will not follow him blindly until the abyss swallows them up.'

I kept my eyes fixed on his face. 'You don't believe that Hannibal will win this war?'

Instead of answering, and without lowering his voice, Silenos said, 'He carries poison about with him.'

Then I confessed to him that I knew about the poison, and I told him also the dream that Hannibal had confided in me after the ride over the Pyrenees. 'The second secret that he shared with me.'

'He cares very much for you, you little Carthaginian,' said Silenos, with no mockery in his voice.

And yet he didn't even notice my leaving the tent, I thought. I just wasn't there for him. With horror I remembered the gaping slit under the left half of his forehead.

Then Silenos said something that startled me into attention. 'I am bound to him,' he said into the tense silence. 'I know that I shall never be able to free myself from him,' he went on as I looked at him in bewilderment. 'He is my fate.'

'He has robbed me of my father and mother and brother, and

196

of Saguntum,' I answered. 'He's taken Carthalo and Suru away from me. Because of him I have no one left.'

'He can't take them all away from you if you don't separate yourself from them,' Silenos assured me.

'But everyone who belonged to me is dead,' I said bitterly, 'except you, and you're going with him. He killed Suru with his own hands.'

'Suru is the one of all of them you will be least able to lose,' Silenos went on unperturbed. 'He will always be walking behind you, even although he's now lying on the hill where his strength at last failed him. Suru is your fate just as Hannibal is mine.'

I tried to raise myself, but Silenos told me to lie still. He looked at the bandage which was soaked through with blood. Then he set to work to take it off. It hurt me. He put a large piece of plaster with healing ointment on it right over the wound and then bound it up with the greatest care. 'It will soon be well,' he assured me. 'It isn't half as bad as it looked at first. But you ought to go to sleep now.'

The wound didn't hurt any more now. 'What did you mean by what you said about Suru?' I asked.

Silenos was making a mixture for me to drink. 'It will taste bitter,' he said when he brought me the bowl. 'But it will make you sleep.'

I refused the drink and repeated my question.

Then Silenos put the bowl aside and began to talk about Suru in a low voice. He tried to quieten me down by what he said. He reminded me now of the subject of our first conversation at the elephants' ford, of the forests under the roof of the world where Suru grew up, of the ravines overflowing with vegetation, of the almond flowers larger than butterflies, of the moonlit nights when yaks and rabbits play on carpets of moss under gigantic trees, and when the elephants dance, enchanted by the moon, until at last they go with the moon into the heart of the jungle, as softly as clouds moving into the dark regions of the sky. 'Suru has a long journey before him—back to his beginning,

197

back over mountains and ice, over deserts and rivers and flowering lands. Everyone who starts off on the great adventure which the Indians call *Mahaprasthan* has to make that journey. But don't be anxious: he will come back. There are no greater travellers anywhere in the world than the elephants; they are always on the move, and always in contact with one another. You know that they send one another messages, and you may be sure that Suru will come back to you, when once he has got used to his new life. You must give him time; he has much to do. He must strip off the fetters which they have put on him, and he must get rid of the shining cross that rises up out of his gigantic head. When he has got over all his wounds he will present himself to you, for you are his Indos; he chose you for himself, and you never wanted anything else but to march with him.'

Someone outside the tent was calling Silenos. He went out.

'I must go to Hannibal,' he said when he came back. 'He wants to dictate to me.' He took his writing materials. 'Drink what's in the bowl,' he said; 'then you will sleep.' He bent over me. 'Stay with me till the wound has healed,' he whispered to me; 'only till then!'

Then he went to Hannibal.

33

Now I was alone. I sipped a little of the drink. It tasted bitter and I left the rest. The wound wasn't hurting any more. My eyes fell on the dagger that Carthalo had given me. It was hanging from one of the tent-posts. I began to think hard. With that dagger Carthalo had given Suru a wound in order to heal him. I kept my eyes fixed on the dagger.

And then I got up. I took the dagger and went out of the tent. There were stars in the sky and no moon. The night was dark and warm. Without stopping to think I began to walk. When I

198

left the camp I wasn't challenged. There were only a few sentries—there was no enemy left.

I had nothing to carry except the dagger and I walked along easily. My arm hardly hurt at all; it was as if I hadn't been wounded. Now that I had set out on my way to look for Suru all my unrest had vanished. I was so sure that I would find him that I took my time. I only needed to walk to the lake, the edge of which had been covered with mist that morning, and then to climb the hill—and he would be there. I walked without looking about me. I walked like that for half the night. Then the moon, a red sickle, came up over the horizon, and I saw the lake. It was covered with thin streaks of mist and was shimmering. And there was the hill too. I walked up it.

I saw Suru lying there. His head and his enormous body stood out against the night sky. Above his head I saw a little cross sparkling—Hannibal's sword. The pommel gave out a cold glitter. Then I dropped my dagger. I ran up the hill to seize Hannibal's weapon. When I put out my hand to take it I fell and hit my shoulder and head on the rock—as large as an elephant—that lay on the hill. Over the top of it I saw the stars shining.

My wound began to hurt again. I picked myself up and went on my way again with increasing speed. I wanted to get to the next hill by the lakeside. The moon was climbing higher in the sky. I was bewildered now and looked down at the mist. Dark shapes rose out of it. It was a swamp lying there under the mist, not a lake. I didn't know where to go, and walked on without an aim. The pain in my arm grew worse. I felt hot and my temples were burning. The moon turned silvery-white and threw shimmering veils over the land as far as I could see.

I was tired, but I couldn't stop walking. When I came to a path I followed it. Suddenly I felt quite certain that I was near Suru.

And then I heard his familiar footsteps behind me. I didn't dare to look round, but now I was walking once again as I had always walked when Suru was behind me—without haste.

When I was sure that he was keeping behind me I began to talk to him. 'I ought to have fled with you long ago,' I said, reproaching myself.

He didn't agree with me. 'It would have come to nothing. Hannibal would have sent Maharbal after us. And even if our flight had been successful the Romans would have caught us. And what then? But as it is now, no one can do us any harm.'

'Where are you going to?' I asked him.

'You know the answer to that,' he said. 'I must first get rid of the fetters on my feet and the shining cross above my head. I am going back the way I came—over mountains and rivers, across deserts and flowering lands, till I find myself under the roof of the world.' Suru was repeating word for word what Silenos had said to me.

'And what then?' I asked.

'Then I shall come again,' I heard him say. 'I shall report to you. Only you mustn't lose patience and run away from me. I must first get used to my new conditions—like you. You can depend on me. Didn't they tell you that I walked behind you when I had no strength left to walk with?'

I confirmed this. 'Silenos told me, and Hannibal told me too.' I stopped short. 'What will you say to Hannibal?'

I heard a low groan behind me. Everything that Suru did was quiet; his words and his footsteps were only just audible, and only someone who knew him as well as I did could make any sense of his words.

'What about Hannibal?' I asked again.

'At first I liked him. I liked his eyes, and I liked the way he spoke. I liked him for having Barmokar and Myrkan untied from the whipping-posts, and for going back to help the timid ones over the Ebro. I admired the way he behaved when we were climbing up to the pass, and I liked him for picking you up when you were at the end of your tether. I liked him for many things, most of all for leaving Arba behind with her little one, because otherwise Arba would also——'

Now Suru stopped short.

'But what about Saguntum and the six thousand, when he ordered the Romans to be picked out?' I reminded him.

'I was just coming to them. You did well to leave him. You couldn't go any farther with him. Besides he has done you a lot of harm. He has robbed you of your father and mother and brother. And he wanted to take me away from you, from the very beginning, but I didn't know that any more than you did. There was so much that I didn't know. Only when one of his eyes was hurt so that he couldn't hide things any more with it, did I recognize the kind of man he was. Hannibal wanted me to go on being his elephant. But you know: I am your elephant.'

It was so easy to talk to Suru. He understood me as so far only Silenos had understood me—perhaps even better. 'And what is to happen now to you and me?'

'There will be a difficulty,' Suru confessed frankly. 'I have a long way to go, but that doesn't alter the fact that I shall be on my way to you.'

'I don't understand that,' I said. 'You must explain it to me; it's very important for me.'

'The simplest way will be for you to think of it as a round-about way. You may be quite sure that I'll come back. Wherever you may be I will find you. Don't forget that I found you in the midst of smoking ruins, when there was hardly anything to be seen of you.'

Then I tried surreptitiously to take a look at Suru. I looked round over my wounded shoulder. He was as near as he used to be, and he again took up half the sky. But now instead of the cluster of reddish rods on his head there was still the cross with the shining pommel.

'We shall get rid of that in time,' said Suru comfortingly, as ir he had heard my thoughts. 'That cold flashing thing will disappear. But you must have patience with me; it can't be done overnight.'

I was giddy with looking round, and it was getting difficult to keep up with Suru. He was pushing me on from behind.

'I can't go on,' I said breathlessly; 'you're walking too quickly.'

Suru apologized and said it was because of the long road that lay before him. 'Turn off the road! Sit down by the wayside! Or better still, lie down and keep quiet, as Silenos said. Silenos! He always understood you and me. He belongs to us, not to Hannibal, even although he's in Hannibal's tent now.'

I turned aside staggering and fell into the hollow by the side of the track where I lay still.

'Stay here quietly and see to it that you get your strength back. It's like it was when we were climbing up to the pass; you must get over the difficulties. I know that you will; I know you well enough to know that you will. We've been through too much together. You will get through. I shall soon be with you again.'

His powerful body pushed past me. The sky grew darker; Suru had taken the stars away with him.

34

WHEN I woke up it was no longer night. I heard the clatter of horses' hoofs and a clanking noise—it was that that had woken me up. It was some time before I collected my wits; my head was turning round, and my first thought was: now it's beginning again, the clatter of the rear-guard and of the Roman legions, and the noise that the Berserkers make. The trap has been laid again. But then my thoughts went on: why, of course, the Romans have all been killed or sifted out and made into slaves, 'which is what they deserve'. These thoughts were mixed with horror and I crouched down in the hollow so that I shouldn't see anything.

The clanking noise and the clatter of hoofs stopped, both quite near me, and then I heard a man cursing. I started up.

Barely five paces away from me I saw a man with two

donkeys. The donkeys had taken fright and the man who was holding them by long reins was trying to quieten them. Each donkey was loaded with two cauldrons, which were black all round and only shone at their rims. Several times again the two nervous beasts of burden ran into one another so that the cauldrons clashed together. At last the donkeys grew quiet.

Then the man called out something to me which I didn't understand, but I knew by his face that it was unfriendly. He tried in another language, and this I knew because he now spoke hesitatingly. And then he began to curse in Roman, and when he saw that I understood he said scoldingly, 'It was you who frightened the donkeys. Whatever made you choose this place to lie in?'

I didn't answer his question—what could I have said? My eyes moved from the man to the two donkeys. I had seen donkeys with baskets on their backs, or pitchers, but donkeys with black cauldrons . . . ?

The man saw that I was puzzled. 'I am a cook,' he explained, 'and this is my kitchen. It travels with me wherever I go. I have cooked for many people—lately for Romans. But now it's all up with them. This Hannibal has sifted the poor devils. He let me go because I'm not a Roman. At the moment I wouldn't advise you to be a Roman.' The man was talking in a jargon of his own, but as he also talked with his hands, and as his face was very expressive, I could follow him.

'And you?' he asked. He came a few steps nearer to me. 'Oh, you've caught it!' he said. Now he tied the donkeys to a tree and looked at me more closely.

'Does it hurt?'

I shook my head.

'These things nearly always look worse than they are,' he said consolingly. 'I can see by looking at you that you're going to get over it. I can tell that with everyone. Where do you come from?'

'From Saguntum,' I said.

He wrinkled his brow. 'Saguntum, where is that?' He had never heard of Saguntum.

'The war is because of Saguntum,' I explained.

The cook was surprised. 'They told me it was because the Carthaginians wanted to get the whole of Rome into their power—the whole world.' He examined me more closely. 'Are you a Carthaginian? You can tell me.'

'They took me with them,' I told him, 'but now I've run away from them.'

His face took on a doubtful expression. 'Then take good care that they don't catch you.' He thought hard. Suddenly he looked very perplexed. 'But your clothes? What did you do when you were with the Carthaginians?'

'I was with the elephants,' I said.

The man looked alarmed.

'The elephants are all dead,' I said to reassure him, 'and most of the drivers, each of which had his elephant—I Suru.'

'You are Suru?' he asked, delighted. 'I am Dukar,' he said, introducing himself. He took a piece of bread out of his pocket and gave it to me. 'Eat, little Suru!' he urged me. 'But what am I going to do with you? Where do you want to go to?'

'To Saguntum,' I said.

'Is it far?' he asked.

'It's in Iberia, by the sea.'

He looked at me incredulously. 'So far? Why, there are mountains in between! But of course you must go home to your father and mother.'

'They're dead. I haven't anyone left,' I said.

'But still you want to go back?' He shook his head vigorously. His mind was made up. 'You're coming with me,' he said. 'I will make a cook of you. Look where you ended up as an elephant-driver. Mercenaries, horse troops, everyone who has anything to do with fighting—they all come to naught. Sooner or later they all have to go to the front and there one kills the other. But with a cook it's different. They keep him as far as possible in the rear. Everyone sees to it that nothing happens to

205

him, because they all want to eat, even if they've just killed other men. Why did I come out alive? Because I'm a cook. And my advice to you is to become a cook. You'll be all right then, whether it's peace or war. I'll teach you to cook,' he volunteered. 'You'll learn it from me in the twinkling of an eye.'

I had raised myself into a sitting position, and now I stood up and took a few steps.

'You see! You can walk,' Dukar cried joyfully. 'And luckily it isn't very far from here to where I live. In any case it's not so far as this——'

'Saguntum,' I said.

'I just can't remember the name of that place,' he said apologetically. 'Very well then, let us start!'

I stood there irresolutely. Dukar didn't seem to be a bad man. Why shouldn't I go with him? Why not let him teach me to cook? But something was holding me back.

'Don't you want to come with me?' He looked at me and it was clear that he was disappointed.

'What will they say to you at home if you take me back with you?' I asked him.

He puffed out his chest. 'Whatever she may say—there'll be two of us now.'

'I don't quite understand,' I said.

Then he came out with a confession. 'You must come with me,' he explained in a pleading tone. 'You can't leave me in the lurch. I just can't manage her alone.' In answer to my amazed expression he told me that he was afraid of going home. 'She doesn't know anything about cooking,' he said, 'but she fancies she can cook better than me. From the very first day there's been nothing but quarrelling between us over this. I ought not to have married her—but who could foretell that? She has quite a presentable face; she isn't bad in other ways—she even has a heart—but her fists are damned hard.

'In the whole war,' Dukar declared, 'I haven't had so many bruises on my back as in one week at home. It mustn't go on any longer. We two together will make her see reason.' He untied

one of the donkeys. 'Take this one!' he declared solemnly. 'He shall be yours if you come with me, as well as the two cauldrons.' He lifted up one cauldron from the saddle so that I could see inside it. Its inside was shining. Then I went with him.

We walked for half the day along by-paths. Then we rested. Dukar cooked; he had still a small stock of provisions with him, and the food he prepared tasted better than anything I had had to eat for a whole year. We avoided the farms. Dukar knew exactly which paths to take.

'We must get out of this district as quickly as possible,' he said, 'so that you don't fall into the hands of the Carthaginians. They will recognize you from afar by your accursed tunic.'

Evening was coming on when we heard the quick clatter of horses' hoofs behind us. A mounted troop was on our track. We stood still behind our donkeys and watched the horsemen coming nearer.

'Your accursed tunic!' muttered Dukar. 'It will bring the Carthaginians down on us.'

I looked steadily at the troop. 'They aren't Carthaginians,' I said when I was quite sure.

'You're right,' said Dukar, 'it's an isolated troop of Romans.' And now he quite lost control of himself. 'Tear your accursed tunic up!'

But now the troop had come up to us. There were six men. Two of them dismounted from their horses and fell upon us with such violence that the donkeys shied.

'What have you got there?' they shouted to Dukar, rapping the cauldrons.

'I'm a cook,' Dukar explained to them. He told them the name of the maniple for which he had cooked. 'But that maniple doesn't exist any longer.'

'But we do,' said the leader. He exchanged looks with the other horsemen. 'He might be useful to us,' said one of them.

Dukar was taken aback. His eyes moved from one donkey to the other.

'And he?' The leader pointed to me.

208

'He's my assistant,' said Dukar uncomfortably.

'Since when?' The leader was getting suspicious. 'What's that tunic he's wearing?' He studied my face. Then he took hold of me by the wounded arm. 'What have you done with your Lucanian ox?' he asked, and his eyes began to glitter. My arm was hurting me so much that I let out a cry of pain. Drops of sweat broke out on my forehead.

'He is wounded,' said Dukar.

'You attend to your donkeys,' the Roman shouted at him roughly, 'or we shall make short work of you too!'

Dukar went up to the leader and with trembling hands besought him: 'He's run away from them—he didn't want to have anything more to do with them, he's still only a boy, and he isn't a Carthaginian, they just carried him off with them. Look how young he is!'

'Stop talking nonsense!' the Roman said warningly.

'He comes from——' Dukar tried desperately to remember the name.

'Saguntum.' I could hardly say the word because of the choking sensation in my throat.

'From Saguntum?' The Roman let my arm go. There was blood on his hand. 'That can't be true, and I'll tell you why. Not a single man, woman, or child who lived in Saguntum is alive today. The devil in the red cloak had them all killed. But we shall find out where you come from. We'll get everything out of you. You will tell us too what you know about elephants. And what *is* your name?'

'Suru,' said Dukar when he saw that I was choking.

'Not you!' the Roman said roughly. 'This one!'

'I am Dukar, the cook,' said Dukar obligingly; 'he is Suru and comes from Saguntum.'

'There isn't such a name in the whole of Iberia,' the Roman told him. 'I was in Iberia quite long enough—no one is called that there.' He ordered us to follow him. The horsemen put us in the middle. After three hours we came to a wood in which about fifty more Romans were hiding.

The cook had a warm welcome. I was shown round like a
strange animal. And then the idea came to the leader to put me
up for sale. 'All that remains of Hannibal's elephants!' he cried.
'Who would like him?'

Someone bid twopence, another three, a third five. They bid
against one another more and more eagerly, till at last the sum
had almost risen to what one would have to pay for a horse.

The man to whom I fell looked me carefully all over.

'What can you do?' he asked me.

'He knows something about elephants!' the leader cried to him. 'You'll get a lot of money for him in Rome. His name is said to be Suru.'

'Suru?' the man repeated to make sure.

My mind was in such confusion that I nodded.

The man looked anxiously at my bandage. He called someone else, who seemed to know something about such matters, and who declared that the bandage had been well put on. The Roman gave me something to eat and drink; he gave me a blanket and insisted that I should rest.

'I must take care of you so that we pull you through,' he explained to me. 'I paid a high price for you.'

When night fell we moved on. The Romans planned to fight their way through to Rome.

'How old are you?' the man to whom I belonged asked me on the way.

'Thirteen,' I said.

The man was astonished. 'And you marched with Hannibal over the Alps?'

'Yes,' said I.

'And that was the end of the elephants' march!' he cried, looking as though he himself had finished off all Hannibal's elephants.

The Treasure

'AND did you get through—to Rome?'

'It took us some time,' said the old man, 'but we got through. The Carthaginians didn't catch us. The Romans knew the paths and secret by-ways—they even got the cook and the donkeys through. It wasn't a bad time because Dukar cooked well, and that kept everyone in a good mood, and as the man to whom I now belonged had nothing against my helping Dukar I could cook after a fashion by the time we got to Rome.' The old man poked the fire with the only branch that was left. All night long he had fed it with little pieces of wood. Now that it was getting light the red glow had died down. He put the bough where it caught fire. Morik and Tana and the old man were all a little cold. He was looking out for the sun.

'It must come up soon,' he said, 'and as soon as it's up we'll open the trap-door.'

'And you couldn't escape from them?' asked Tana.

'Where to?' asked the old man in his turn. 'I shouldn't have got far with that wound. Besides, I didn't want to escape while Dukar was with us. And the man who had bought me kept a very strict watch over me, and over my wound, and even my driver's tunic. He had realized how valuable I was. And in fact he did make a lot of money out of me. I was shown in all the public places of Rome. The Romans crowded round me; they had trembled before Hannibal's elephants, and now they didn't exist any more. I was all that was left of them. A rich Roman bought me and paid a good price to become the owner of Suru— the last remnant of Hannibal's elephants.'

Morik, whose ideas about the old man had changed during the night, hesitated before he said, 'And didn't they try to get anything out of you—about the elephants?'

213

The old man smiled indulgently. 'You don't know the Romans. What they intend to do they do. But why talk about it?'

'They tortured you?' asked Tana in horror.

'Why should I escape what Carthalo had to undergo?' said the old man calmly. 'As you see, I survived it. It was only bad at first, when I had no one but myself to depend on. But then suddenly Carthalo was standing beside me and he kept on charging me, "Don't say anything to them, or at least nothing true. Do as I did, lie to them; they won't know you're lying." He showed me the brand they had burnt on his wrist. "Now you'll have one too! Do you believe now what I said: that they're devils and that one must hate them?" I bit my lips till they bled and said nothing. They wanted me to tell them everything I knew about elephants, particularly where to strike if you want to kill them quickly. I said nothing. I lay there and felt as powerless to move as that time when I lay buried in the rubble of Saguntum. They had tied me on to the rack. Just as I was going to speak and to lie to them as Carthalo did, Suru appeared before me and Carthalo vanished. This time Suru had the bunch of red rods on his head again as at Saguntum. The glittering cross had gone. He was holding his head to one side. "Tell them everything," he advised me. "Don't lie to them! Tell them what they want to know and then they will leave you in peace." And then I talked—until I had told them everything I knew about elephants.'

'And they let you go?' asked Tana.

'Later,' said the old man. 'About forty or fifty years later. I have given up counting the years.'

'It's impossible not to hate them!' cried Morik angrily.

The old man shook his head. 'Carthalo hated them and he died of his hatred. I was thankful when they left me in peace. And now I had Suru again. He had come back to me at the right moment. Without him I could never have held out, but he wanted me to come through. And now whenever I felt inclined to talk I had some one to talk to again. What more could I want?'

214

'And what happened to Hannibal after that?' Morik asked.

'I thought you would be more interested in him than in Suru.' The old man let it appear that he was offended by Morik's question. He looked towards the mountains in the east. The sky above them was pink. 'The sun will be up soon,' said the old man, 'and then we will open the trap-door.'

'One more question,' said Morik. 'Did you ever see Hannibal again?'

'Hannibal?' The old man made a disdainful gesture. 'I hadn't wanted to have anything more to do with him. But I came across him at every turn. In every street in Rome, wherever men talked together, he haunted their conversation; he even haunted their dreams. I too dreamt of him. He was taking vengeance upon me for having run away from him. The legions that Rome raised against him were of no avail. No one knew how to wage war as he did. Once when he was in the mountains he fell into a trap. He tied bunches of twigs on to the horns of a herd of cattle, and ordered them to be set alight, when he had moved up to the pass over which he intended to escape. The blazing fires which came rushing along in the darkness created a panic among the Romans, and Hannibal escaped. He won victory after victory, but the war went on. When they saw that the Consuls could not defeat Hannibal, the Romans put up a dictator against him. But this dictator was a man who didn't believe in decisive battles. He was called the Waverer. Year after year he marched alongside of Hannibal instead of bringing him to a stand. Hannibal had no peace. The Carthaginians caught fevers and melted away. The perpetual marching round and round softened them. The Waverer had invented a kind of war in which Hannibal was never able to make a move. By doing nothing he made the Carthaginians the losers. But there were Romans who accused the Waverer of cowardice, and some even called him a traitor. So now again they sent Consuls against Hannibal, and one, a butcher's son named Varro, planned to take him by the throat. In Apulia, at Cannae, he brought the Carthaginians to a stand, and now at last Hannibal had again the kind of war that he excelled in. He caught the Romans in a worse pincer-grip than by the Trebia or by Lake Trasimenus, so that the burning summer sun blinded them and the dust choked them, and in the end more than fifty thousand Romans lay dead on the field of blood. Now Rome called half-grown boys and slaves to arms; allies who had deserted the Romans were either driven into battle against Hannibal or made into slaves. Syracuse, which sided with Hannibal, was conquered, although a famous Syracusan called Archimedes had invented an enormous pair of iron hands with which the defenders of a city, standing on the walls, could seize and lift up soldiers and even ships. When Hannibal appeared before Rome and set up his camp there, the fields on which the tents of the Carthaginians stood were bought and sold in Rome at their full price. And then I saw the man in the red cloak again—for the last time and only from a distance. They had put my driver's tunic on me and showed me to the Carthaginians from the wall: "So it shall be with all of you! In everyone of you a slave lies hidden!" Hannibal had to withdraw. And when his brother Hasdrubal set out from Iberia to come to his help his army was captured and destroyed, down to the last man and the last elephant, and Hasdrubal's head was flung from a pole into Hannibal's camp. Now Hannibal knew that the hour had struck. After seventeen years of war had brought death to countless men, destruction to four hundred towns, and immeasurable devastation to the whole country, Hannibal found himself obliged to return to Africa. A Roman army had landed there and was threatening Carthage. The Carthaginians had sent ships for Hannibal—but not many ships. He gave the order to slay all those for whom there was no room on the ships: all the horses and all the auxiliaries. Then he put up a brass tablet in the temple of Hercules in Croton on which his victories were engraved, and sailed to Carthage. At Zama the Romans brought him to bay and killed or captured those mercenaries who had followed him loyally over the Alps and over the sea to Carthage. Hannibal was beaten. The victor was Publius Cornelius Scipio, who as a seventeen-year-old boy had cut a way of escape for his father out of the thick of the fighting in the battle by the River Ticino, and as a twenty-five-year-old man had conquered New Carthage when an unusually low tide had made it possible to attack the city from the coast. And now this Scipio captured five hundred Carthaginian ships and had them burnt. He took all but thirty of their elephants and returned to Rome as Scipio Africanus with the elephants. He took drivers for them also. The Roman to whom I now belonged was a patriot like other Romans and put me at the disposal of the elephants' masters. "Lucanian oxen!" the Romans roared, when the elephants were led through the city. Now that they had brought Carthage low their fear of the elephants had vanished. They gave everything that came out of Africa boastfully insulting names. They called leopards African rats and ostriches sea-sparrows because they had been brought across the sea to Rome. And they had no intention of using the elephants for their legions. "To the circus with them!" they cried. The elephants were taught to walk upstairs, to eat off plates, and to carry candlesticks. The Romans wanted to laugh at the Lucanian oxen who had once aroused such terror in them. They wanted to deride Carthage in the person of the elephants. Carthage was still there. The Carthaginians were forbidden to make war without Rome's permission. But nevertheless there was a third war. In Rome there was a man called Cato who had great influence. He hated Carthage, just as Carthalo had hated Rome. But Cato didn't die of his hatred, he made Carthage die of it. He deliberately started the war under some pretext or other. Carthage submitted. It handed over all its weapons, elephants, and ships. Only then did Cato tell the Carthaginians that their city would disappear from the face of the earth and that they were to build themselves a new city a three hours' journey from the coast. In desperation the Carthaginians decided that although they had no weapons they would fight to the end. In feverish haste they forged weapons out of tools. Out of bowls, scissors, fish-hooks, spoons, and knives, they made in the shortest possible time three thousand shields, nine thousand swords, fifteen thousand spears, and thirty thousand arrows.

The women gave their hair and bow-strings were made out of it. They fought for three years till hunger turned them into shadows. Then they set fire to their city, which meant more to them than their own lives. I had been taken to Africa with a company of other drivers. The Romans believed the Carthaginians to be capable of any devilish trick—even that they had kept elephants in hiding in the city, although at the conclusion of the armistice every corner was searched for elephants. I saw Carthage burning. The shining ship of stone was turned like Saguntum into a smoking heap of rubble. I saw Saguntum burning a second time. The pillars between which the ships had lain at anchor fell down in flames; the store of the colour workers at the foot of the Fire Mountain, the fort, the tall dwelling-houses and the palaces were all burnt. When all was over we were sent into the town to look for elephants. This city didn't smell of cedarwood or bakers' wares, nor was there the sound of the ringing of copper under the hammers. I saw a Carthage that Carthalo didn't know. In the walls enormous caves were gaping, the empty stables of the elephants. Not a single elephant was discovered, nor a single living Carthaginian. But I met some men who were now no more than skin and bone and whose eyes nevertheless were shining with joy. They were condemned men who had been seized out of their hell, the slaves from the chalk quarries by the sea. After years of living in hell they were now free and could go where they liked. They embraced me as if I had been their deliverer. In the general confusion there was nothing to distinguish one man from another. Then I also set out on my way. I walked westward, through the gardens of Megara, and then farther along the coast. I walked by the elephants' road as far as the Pillars of Hercules. A ship took me across the sea to Gades in return for a handful of coins which I had found in a street in Carthage. I was in Iberia. It belonged to the Romans now. No one stopped me. An old man with not long to live— what harm can he do? They didn't know that I was the only man left who knew every hole and corner of Saguntum, who knew where digging would be worth while.' The old man

218

stretched out his right arm and pointed to the mountains in the east. 'It will be up any minute now!' The mountains were already sharply outlined.

Morik was looking closely at the old man's arm. He could see no signs of a brand. 'Didn't they brand you then?' he asked without stopping to think.

The old man held out his wrist to him. 'Here.' He pointed to a scar. 'As time has gone on and as I grew old it has almost disappeared. I didn't hide it like Carthalo; the sun and wind could get at it. Time has wiped it out—because I didn't stop living. Hannibal gave up,' he declared angrily. But then he began to defend him. 'His own people gave him the worst blows. They wanted to bring him to trial for "deliberately abstaining from the conquest of Rome". He fled from country to country; his house in Carthage was razed to the ground by Carthaginians, and after the Romans had made a demand for his surrender for the fifth time he was driven to use the phial in his belt. He died of poison.'

'And Silenos, what happened to him?' asked Tana.

'I met him several times later,' said the old man with a more cheerful expression on his face. 'In the house of the rich man who had finally bought me there were books. One day, many years after the Hannibal war, the man brought a new book home; it was Silenos. The man had friends with whom he discussed his books. He thought very highly of Silenos, "because he was there and must know how things happened". We lived together under the same roof for several years—Silenos and I.'

Then Morik asked, 'What *is* your name? We know so much about you, and don't know what you are called.'

'You can safely call me Suru,' said the old man with a secret smile. He blinked. And then they noticed that the sun was up. The wall behind the old man was lit up.

'Now it's light enough!' he cried. 'Now we shall see it sparkling down below there. We will open it.'

Morik and Tana both wanted to help the old man to stand up. He refused their help and propped himself against the little wall that he had built himself.

219

'Someone is coming,' he said, looking out over the wall.

'It's Father,' said Tana.

'Why must he come just now?' muttered Morik, annoyed.

They watched him coming without moving. He found a tense silence when he arrived.

'You're not digging!' he said reproachfully.

'We're through,' said the old man in a friendly tone.

'And you didn't fetch me?' Their father looked at Morik and Tana suspiciously.

'We were as far as this yesterday,' Morik confessed, 'soon after it got dark.'

'And what have you been doing all night?'

'Suru was telling us his story.'

'Why?' asked their father indignantly. 'If there's anything down there, why wait to tell stories about it?'

'Suru wanted it to sparkle when we open up,' Tana explained.

Then their father strode impatiently towards the old man. 'Old man,' he said, 'don't run away with the idea that everything down there belongs to you.'

'I don't want it only for myself,' said the old man calmly. 'You will have your share.'

'How much?' asked their father in a blustering tone.

'As much as you like.'

Their father insisted that they should settle beforehand how much each was to have. 'We are four,' he said, 'you are only one. But let us put the two children together and make one of them— then we are three and you one. A quarter for you, three-quarters for us, do you agree?'

'You're very precise,' said the old man mockingly.

'You haven't got much longer to live, remember that!' their father said.

'Right!' said the old man. 'But then you might at least help me build my house.'

'That we will do,' their father promised, and his eyes shone with joy at the thought that he would have three-quarters for

220

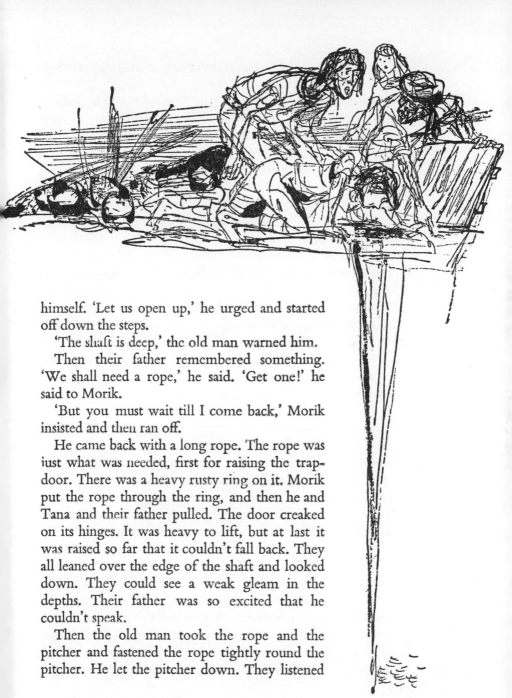

himself. 'Let us open up,' he urged and started
off down the steps.

'The shaft is deep,' the old man warned him.

Then their father remembered something.
'We shall need a rope,' he said. 'Get one!' he
said to Morik.

'But you must wait till I come back,' Morik
insisted and then ran off.

He came back with a long rope. The rope was
just what was needed, first for raising the trap-
door. There was a heavy rusty ring on it. Morik
put the rope through the ring, and then he and
Tana and their father pulled. The door creaked
on its hinges. It was heavy to lift, but at last it
was raised so far that it couldn't fall back. They
all leaned over the edge of the shaft and looked
down. They could see a weak gleam in the
depths. Their father was so excited that he
couldn't speak.

Then the old man took the rope and the
pitcher and fastened the rope tightly round the
pitcher. He let the pitcher down. They listened

holding their breath. When a splashing sound reached them their father sprang up.

'Water!' he yelled at the old man. 'If it's deep, how shall we get to the treasure?'

'It's deeper than the height of a house,' said the old man, drawing up the pitcher.

'How do you know that?' asked their father in great excitement.

The pitcher came into view. It was full of water. The old man drank. His face showed how moved he was.

'Drink,' he said; 'you won't find better water anywhere in the world.'

Their father was the first to understand. 'Do you mean to say that it's an ordinary well?'

The old man looked at him. 'Is that nothing?' he asked.

'Yes, of course, a well is useful.' Their father was finding it difficult to control himself. 'But where is the shaft into which they threw their treasures? If you knew the well was here you must also know where the shaft is.'

'I know exactly where it is,' said the old man.

'Let us go to it,' their father urged.

The old man gave him a pitying look. 'Someone has been there before us—Hannibal. He plundered Saguntum. And he had everything that was in the shaft dug up for himself, for his war treasury. He bought mercenaries with it.'

'Moloch take him!' Their father began to curse.

'You may be sure that not a single coin was left in the shaft,' said the old man. And now suddenly he felt for the little leather bag which was hanging round his neck and looked inside it. He took out a coin and handed it to Tana and Morik. 'There it is —I've kept it safe from Hannibal and also from the Romans.'

Tana and Morik examined the insignificant-looking coin, on which they could just make out a palm-tree.

'They let me keep it because it was worth so little—to them, but not to me. I don't want any other. I don't even polish it, I want it to stay like it was when he gave it to me.'

222

'What are you three talking about?' their father asked.

'We're talking about Suru,' answered Morik.

'You have a name that I've never heard before,' said their father in an unfriendly tone.

'Will you nevertheless help me with the house?'

Their father gave him a spiteful look. 'So you need a house now? You're as old as'—he was trying to find the right word—'an elephant.'

The old man laughed and held his head a little to one side. 'Do I look like one?' he cried, delighted. 'Very well then, call me an elephant! I shall soon have lived as long as an elephant lives anyhow. And, let me tell you, elephants are well-diggers; they know where water is to be found underground. Suru knew that there would be water here.' Now he was serious again. 'This is better water than at the fort—try it!' he urged their father.

And now their father took the pitcher and drank.

'You're right,' he agreed. 'It's better than at the fort, and not so far.'

'And there's plenty of it,' said the old man joyfully. 'Half Saguntum used to draw water here. You won't have to go away now. One can live here. Is that nothing?'

'We'll build our house here,' said their father, more to himself than to the others.

'And my house?' the old man asked.

'You shall have it, you old elephant!' Their father was leaning on the trap-door and looking into the shaft, and deep down he saw the water sparkling.

Chronological Table

753   (or 814 B.C.) Foundation of Rome by Romulus and Remus and of Carthage by Queen Dido (Elissa) of Tyre, capital of Phoenicia.

480   Defeat of the Greeks by the Carthaginians at Himera. Establishment of the Court of the Hundred, who from now on rule Carthage.

275   The Romans see elephants for the first time in the army of Pyrrhus in Lucania (hence the nickname 'Lucanian oxen').

265   The establishment of a pirate state in Messina by the mercenaries who under the Syracusan Agathocles had besieged Carthage but failed to take it.

264   Rome makes an alliance with the 'Mars men' of Messina against Carthage.

264–241 First Punic War, in which Carthage loses Sicily and the dominion of the western Mediterranean. The Roman fleet, partly by reason of its grappling bridges, proves superior to the Carthaginian fleet. In the years after the war, while Carthage is defenceless owing to a mutiny of its mercenaries, Rome takes Sardinia also and raises the war tribute. In this 'irreconcilable war' Hamilcar Barca suppresses the mutiny and in the succeeding years builds a new Carthage in Spain.

247   Birth of Hannibal.

229   (or 228) Death of Hamilcar Barca.

221   His son-in-law and successor Hasdrubal is murdered.

219   (in October) Hannibal destroys Saguntum.

218–202 Second Punic War, 'waged more with hatred than with power' (Livy). In May Hannibal's army of 40,000 men, 6,000 horses, and 39 elephants sets out from New

224

Carthage on its march, has covered about 1,200 kilometres by September, crosses the Rhône, crosses the Alps approximately between the 10th and 25th of October, according to the latest fairly dependable results of research, by the Pass of Traversette. At the end of October the town of the Taurini (Turin) is conquered. After an engagement with horse troops on the banks of the Ticino comes the battle by the Trebia on the 23rd December, in which Hannibal inflicts a devastating defeat on the Romans under the Consuls Scipio and Sempronius. Hannibal loses all the elephants who have survived the crossing of the Alps except one.

217 In the spring Hannibal breaks up his winter camp. After one unsuccessful attempt he crosses the Apennines in May. A second annihilating defeat of the Romans by Lake Trasimenus.

216 The battle of Cannae in which more than 50,000 out of 86,000 Romans are slain. Rome puts sixteen-year-olds and slaves under arms.

212 Syracuse is conquered by the Romans; in the course of fighting a legionary kills Archimedes.

211 Hannibal at the gates of Rome.

209 Twenty-five-year-old Scipio conquers New Carthage.

207 Hasdrubal, hastening to help his brother, is slain, and his army and ten elephants are destroyed.

205 Hannibal puts up a brass tablet on which his victories are engraved in the Temple of Hercules at Croton. He leaves Italy.

202 Scipio Africanus defeats Hannibal at Zama. Carthage is forbidden to make war without the consent of Rome.

183 After the Romans' fifth demand for the surrender of Hannibal he takes poison. ('Let us put an end to the great anxiety of the Romans, since they cannot wait till an old man dies in peace.') Scipio, having quarrelled with Rome, dies in voluntary exile.